LEABHARLANN CHONTAE
LIATROMA
LEITRIM COUNTY LIBRARY

WITHDRAWN FROM STOCK
LEITRIM COUNTY LIBRARY

WITHDRAWN FROM STOCK
LEITRIM COUNTY LIBRARY

HOW TO BE LOST

a novel by

Amanda Eyre Ward

WITHDRAWN FROM STOCK
LEITRIM COUNTY LIBRARY

LEABHARLANN CHONTAE
LIATROMA
LEITRIM COUNTY LIBRARY

WITHDRAWN FROM STOCK
LEITRIM COUNTY LIBRARY

WITHDRAWN FROM STOCK
LEITRIM COUNTY LIBRARY

HOW TO BE LOST

a novel by

Amanda Eyre Ward

Hutchinson
London

Published by Hutchinson in 2005

1 3 5 7 9 10 8 6 4 2

Copyright © Amanda Eyre Ward 2005

Amanda Eyre Ward has asserted her right under the Copyright, Designs and Patents Act, 1988 to be identified as the author of this work

This book is sold subject to the condition that it shall not, by way of trade or otherwise, be lent, resold, hired out, or otherwise circulated without the publisher's prior consent in any form of binding or cover other than that in which it is published and without a similar condition including this condition being imposed on the subsequent purchaser

First published in the United States by MacAdam/Cage Publishing in 2004

Hutchinson
The Random House Group Limited
20 Vauxhall Bridge Road, London SW1V 2SA

Random House Australia (Pty) Limited
20 Alfred Street, Milsons Point, Sydney
New South Wales 2061, Australia

Random House New Zealand Limited
18 Poland Road, Glenfield
Auckland 10, New Zealand

Random House (Pty) Limited
Endulini, 5a Jubilee Road
Parktown 2193, South Africa

The Random House Group Limited Reg. No. 954009

www.randomhouse.co.uk

A CIP catalogue record for this book is available
from the British Library

Papers used by Random House are natural, recyclable products made from wood grown in sustainable forests. The manufacturing processes conform to the environmental regulations of the country of origin

Printed and bound in Great Britain by
Mackays of Chatham Plc, Chatham, Kent

ISBN 0 09 179979 1

For Mary-Anne Westley,
my mother and guiding star

PART ONE

ONE

THE AFTERNOON BEFORE, I planned how I would tell her. I would begin with my age and maturity, allude to a new lover, and finish with a bouquet of promises: grandchildren, handwritten letters, boxes from Tiffany sent in time to beat the rush. I sat in my apartment drinking Scotch and planning the words. "Mom," I said to Georgette, the cat. "Mom, I have something important to discuss."

Georgette stretched lazily on the balcony. Below, an ambulance wailed. A man with a shopping cart stood underneath my apartment building, eating chicken wings and whistling. The heat had dimmed, but the smell of New Orleans seemed to grow stronger: old meat, sweat, and beer.

"Mom," I told the cat, "please listen to what I am telling you." Although Georgette continued to ignore me, the man with the shopping cart looked up, and I took this as a good sign.

I had to work that night, so after the Scotch and a small nap, I stood in front of the mirror and put on mascara. I was going for sultry European, so I took my hair in my fingers and twisted it, securing the roll with bobby pins. Was this a chignon? How did one pronounce *chignon*? In any case, my hair was out of my face, and this would please the health department. I washed my hands with the rose-scented soap my sister had sent me, and slipped my feet into heels. As a final gesture, I drew a mole next to the left corner of my mouth.

We had been told, at The Highball, to "glamorize our images." This is a direct quote. Jimbo, the club's elderly owner, had begun soliciting buyers for his "little piece of New Orleans history." The Highball was the cocktail lounge at the top of the World Trade Center in New Orleans. It revolved. If you sat drinking expensive themed cocktails for a full hour, you would see the whole city, from the lazy Mississippi River to the dilapidated downtown, to the French Quarter, and back again to the mighty Miss, Old Man River.

Jimbo had implored us, in his memo, to glamorize. I believe he thought that despite the old plush décor, despite our advancing ages (I was thirty-two, in a town where many cocktail waitresses were underage runaways) and annoyed demeanors, if we tarted up, he could convince some Yankee that The Highball was an exclusive club, and not a tourist trap that revolved. So, why not? My old look (irritable and overtired) hadn't gotten me many dates. Along with Winnie, I went to Payless Shoes and bought a few pairs of high heels. We bought fishnet stockings and perfume. And then we went to Bobby's Bar and drank beer from giant cans until we ran out of quarters for the jukebox.

I drove slowly to The Highball. With my car windows closed and my air-conditioning on, the night was lovely. People sat on their front steps drinking from paper bags and watching kids play soccer. I was one of the few white people in my neighborhood, and one of the many heavy drinkers. I waved to Lady B, my landlord, who was sitting on her porch swing and braiding her daughter Lela's hair. Lady B winked in response.

Although I didn't have to, I drove up Canal Street, past Harrah's. Three frat boys, their necks strung with beads, sat on the sidewalk outside the casino. Their eyes were glazed, and they were not drinking from their giant daiquiris. They were simply staring at the street, defeated. These were the sorts of people who eventually roused themselves to ride the elevator to The Highball. More than one of my customers had fallen asleep in their velvet chair.

Things were slow up at The H-ball. Winnie was leaning on the bar, her tight dress leaving no inch to the imagination. Behind the bar, Peggy the yoga queen mixed a martini like Tom Cruise, shaking her hips this way and that. A few customers gazed out the window. One couple was making out madly. The good thing about a revolving bar is that odious customers are soon out of sight.

"Look at you!" said Winnie, pointing red fingernails and laughing throatily.

"What?" I said. "It's a chignon."

Winnie and Peggy looked at each other. Sometimes, I surprised them.

It was a long night, and everybody wanted bourbon. When my shift was over, even I wanted bourbon, instead of my usual Scotch. Peggy poured me a stiff one. "I am dreading tomorrow," I told her.

"Why?"

"I have to tell my mother I'm not coming home for Christmas. She's going to flip."

Peggy sat down on her stool. She had removed every bit of her eyebrows, and drawn thin lines. "Why not?" she said.

"What?"

"Why aren't you going home?" said Peggy. She poured herself a glass of bourbon.

"Oh, it's a long story," I said. "For one thing, I'm an adult, you know? I can't go flying home to New York for every holiday like I'm in college or something."

"I never went to college," Peggy said, dreamily.

"And my family…well, it's a bit fucked up, is the thing," I said.

"I wonder," said Peggy.

"What?"

Peggy sipped her drink, and looked through the enormous windows at the sparkling city below. "I wonder who I would be," she said, "if I had gone to college."

"I went to college," I said, "and I'm still here."

Peggy nodded. "But you're you," she said.

On the drive home, I fantasized about my Christmas alone. I would buy a little tree for my apartment and decorate it with lights. I could spend the day at the movies, or at the

Napoleon House, eating a muffaleta sandwich and then slowly drinking my way through a bottle of house red. Winnie had already invited me over for turkey, and I could watch all the kids at her house open presents. Or I could work on Christmas, and make a bundle. Jimbo paid double on holidays.

I wouldn't have to hear it from my sister Madeline and her investment banker husband, Ron. And the Christmas party. My mother insisted on keeping up the Christmas party tradition, making us don taffeta dresses, hiring the bartender from the Liquor Barn. She made the same meatballs, a little too sweet, and the cheese ball. The cheese ball! There must have been a time when an enormous mass of orange and pink cheese covered with nuts and parsley was fashionable, and my mother has not moved past that time. My mother, who was a model in the sixties, who loved fondue, who made cheese balls and laughed so brightly it made me want to cry.

Last year, I wore the costume and deflected questions about my career. ("Just tell them you're still playing," my mother had said, "I beg of you.") I drank too much wine, listened to my brother-in-law's investment advice, and did not argue with Madeline.

I went to sleep before making a scene, but in the middle of the night, I woke up. The guests were gone, and the condo was silent. Next to me, my sister breathed slowly. Strands of hair clung to her flushed cheeks, and she smelled of face cream. I looked at her, the curve of her nose, her thin lips. Her eyelashes, clean of mascara, were pale, and her skin was lightly freckled. In many ways, she was a stranger to me now: an Upper East Side wife, nervous and easily wounded. And yet, in the glow of the streetlamp outside the bedroom, she was the same girl who had once told me *You and me are our family,* her eyes searching mine for a promise. I touched her cheek with my fingers, and she stirred, furrowed her brow, but did not wake.

Our room was on the third floor of my mother's condo, and I went downstairs, past my mother's bedroom and the den, where Ron slept on the pullout couch. (For the first year of their marriage, Madeline had slept with him on the uncomfortable couch at Christmastime, but now she came upstairs to sleep next to me.) I had hoped to find some left-over meatballs, or to make a ham sandwich with the Harrington's maple ham and the little slices of rye bread. I made my way to the kitchen, but as I stepped carefully to avoid waking Ron, I heard something.

I turned toward the sound, and closed my eyes. It was muffled, a sort of breathing. For a moment, I felt a wave of fear, thinking it was a prowler, a robber, murderer, or rapist, but then I remembered I was in suburban New York, and not New Orleans, and my mother's condo complex had a guard-house. I was wearing wool socks and my Christmas nightgown.

My eyes adjusted to the light. In the kitchen, by the sliding glass door that led to the third-story deck, I saw a figure: my mother. "Mom?" I said.

She looked up, and I could see she was crying. "Mom? What is it?"

"Nothing," she said. She blinked quickly and ran the sleeve of her bathrobe across her eyes. By the time I reached her—a few seconds—she was composed. "I was just thinking about Christmas," she said, a false edge of cheer lining her voice. She clutched the picture in her hands. The blurry one, taken on a fall morning a lifetime ago when we had covered Ellie in leaves.

"Oh, Mom," I said.

"No," she said.

"I won't...."

"Caroline," said my mother, her voice grave, "we are talking about Christmas, and only Christmas."

"Mom, it's OK to miss her."

"I hope I get a cashmere sweater," said my mother.

"Mom, we have to talk about this," I said. "She's gone. It's not your fault."

"And maybe some of those cute fur mittens."

From my mother's lap, where she remained trapped in a black-and-white picture, my lost sister looked out at us, laughing.

TWO

THE NEXT MORNING was dull and muggy. December in New Orleans: the thick haze of summer finally dissipated. Georgette rolled over when I sat up in bed. She looked at me steadily. My head felt scraped out and hollow, and it hurt to open my eyes. I lay back down underneath my sheet–it was flowered, a blue print–and wished I had a man to press my skin against. In my apartment, there was only a shadow of the night's coolness. The heat was pushing its way through the windows even before the sun had risen.

I had to call my mother about Christmas, and then I had to glamorize again and serve overpriced drinks to members of the Association of American Lung Surgeons. Every week, a new batch of conference-goers flooded my city and headed, inevitably, to The Highball. As the years went by, we were able to plan ahead: the Amway week was slow, Electrolux salespeople went for champagne. The amazing thing about the Lung people is that they smoked as much as everyone else.

Rubbing my eyes, I promised myself that I would stop drinking alone at night. Outside, there was a crash of metal. I lived at a corner that averaged an accident a month. Whether it was the drinking habits of my neighbors or badly marked streets, it was just depressing.

In the kitchen, I made coffee, spooning the last of the bag into a filter. The kitchen was in the back of the apartment, so I did not have to listen to the aftermath of the collision. The clock on top of the refrigerator read 6:34. My mother would be awake soon, making Toaster-Kakes and covering them with butter. She mixed milk and sugar into her coffee. I drank mine black, in a blue mug that said "#1 Boss," though I'd never been the boss of anyone.

I was thirty-two, and hadn't had a date in a year. Recently, I had begun to think about being on my own forever. As for kids, I was ill equipped. I was impatient, hard-drinking. I spent days in bed with trashy novels, climbing out and pulling on sweats only long enough to grab a bag of Taco Bell (I loved chalupas). What kind of a mother would I be? I worked nights, fantasized about strange men. I ate hot dogs by choice. From the gas station on the corner. Three for a dollar–I ate all three. I was supposed to have become a famous pianist, but was a cocktail waitress instead.

My mother lived in Holt, New York, the town where I grew up. It's a small town, twenty minutes from New York City, on Long Island Sound. If you stood just right, her condo had a view of the water.

While the coffee was brewing (and I did love that sound, as it dripped into the pot), I went to get the paper from my front steps. The *Times-Picayune,* a travesty of a paper, so filled with bad news that it was thrilling to read. The obituaries, especially, interested me. New Orleans had an inordinate amount of death. There were young heroin addicts, middle-aged gunfight victims, elderly ladies who smoked Pall Malls until their dying day.

And there were the Society pages: newly minted queens of Mardi Gras Krewes, debs of the season, benefit galas. Most mornings I read the paper on the balcony, the sun warming my hair. But this morning, I read in the kitchen. I did not want to see the accident. I saw rescue workers with the Jaws of Life prying open a car once, and once was enough.

My coffee was strong and hot. I turned on the ceiling fan, fed Georgette, and settled down to read. The sound of an ambulance became loud and then stopped. On the front page was another damn story about the Saints and their demands for a new stadium. "Absurd," I said to Georgette. The obituaries were at the back of the paper. I finished one cup of coffee and poured another. I looked over a photo spread of some new debutantes frolicking at a pool party, each carrying a towel with her monogram embroidered on it.

The phone rang, and I answered it. "Honey? Caroline?" It was my mother, up early.

"Hi, Mom," I said.

"Oh, Caroline!" My mother sounded close to tears, which was unusual in the morning. Generally, she only grew teary in the evenings, after too many wine spritzers. When my father died of cirrhosis, she cut back on her own drinking, but she still got tipsy most nights.

"What is it?" I said.

"It's your sister. It's Madeline...."

"What?"

"It's that lawyer, the Simpsons' lawyer. They want–" Her voice broke.

"Mom?"

"Oh, Caroline," said my mother. "That horrible man's trial is in January. The one who...."

"Killed Helen Simpson."

"Yes. And they...they think...they think he...." Her voice dropped to a whisper. "Killed Ellie."

"Mom, I know. But what does this have to do with Madeline?"

"She wants closure."

I rubbed my eyes. "You're losing me."

"It's...oh, Caroline!"

"Mom, please. Please calm down. I can't help you if you don't...."

"They want me to say she's dead!"

"They want you to say that Ellie's dead?"

"Y-e-e-sss," said my mother, a strangled assent. I heard her blow her nose.

"Mom, have you been drinking?"

There was silence. "A small Bloody Mary," she admitted.

I sighed. "Can you try to calm down and explain what's going on?"

"Don't yell at me," she sobbed, and then she blew her nose again. "Anyway," said my mother, "we'll discuss it all next week at Christmas."

"Right, ah, Mom, I need to talk to you about that." There was no sound on the New York end of the line. "Mom?"

"Yes?" Her voice was tight.

"The thing is, well...." Visions flashed in my mind: a quiet stroll through the French Quarter, my personal Christmas tree. Georgette stopped licking her paw and looked at me. "I can't make it home this year," I said. I sipped my coffee. "Mom?" I said finally.

Nothing.

"Mom," I said, "I hear you breathing."

"You're coming home for Christmas."

"Well, I have to work, see, and the plane tickets...I mean, we're inside of the fourteen-day advance here. You know, I really think that there comes, um, a time...."

"Do you have a boyfriend?" said my mother, hope like a butterfly in her voice.

"Well, the thing is, Jimbo pays double on...."

"Is there a man in your life?"

"Mom, the thing is...."

"A woman? I'd understand, you know, Caroline."

"Mom! No, there's nobody. It's more that...."

"Oh," said my mother flatly. "Well then, I'll see you on Wednesday."

"Mom, I don't think you're listening."

"The Christmas party is Thursday, and I have the most beautiful red dress for you. And the Royans' son is still single!" She seemed to have regained her usual manic cheer. I didn't have the heart to tell her the Royans' son was gay.

"But Mom, I can't...." She waited me out. "I can't afford

a ticket," I said, finally.

"Caroline," said my mother, "you know I'm paying. And I need you." She sniffled a bit, and I rolled my eyes.

"I'm sorry," I told her, but I could already feel my resolve wavering. "Oh fuck," I said.

"I'll make the cheese ball!" shrieked my mother.

THREE

THE CHRISTMAS PARTY was coming to an end, though *Elvis' Christmas Classics* was still blaring. The bartender from the Liquor Barn was packing up the unopened bottles, someone had stolen the mistletoe, and only a few of the guests were left. Mom, in red-and-black striped pants, held a meatball on a toothpick and nodded seriously, listening to a man in a bow tie describe his boat restoration project. Madeline was putting Saran Wrap around everything that wasn't tied down, pushing the plastic against bowls and platters with concentration. Ron seemed amused by a tall woman's tale of woe at the poodle groomer. "I said one red bow," she exclaimed, "and they made little Keenie's ears into pigtails! Now that is tacky."

Agreeable Ron. He smiled sympathetically.

I had finally extricated myself from a lengthy lecture. Dr. Randall, who had been our pediatrician, was discussing with himself whether Princeton had changed since the day they let ladies in the door. I had no opinion, I said a few dozen times, having never been to Princeton, but Dr. Randall seemed to have enough opinions of his own to keep the conversation going for some time. In conclusion, Dr. Randall finally said, the whole university had gone down the drain–no offense there, Caroline–since females had started meddling.

The bartender saved me. He walked right up, interrupted Dr. Randall's discussion of ladies' lacrosse, and said, "Excuse me, but could you sign the bill?" He was handsome in a swarthy way: black hair, deep blue eyes. His nose was large. "Sorry to interrupt," he said, not looking the least bit sorry.

"Sure. No problem." I smoothed the fabric of my red taffeta dress and rubbed my lips together. Unfortunately, they felt dry, as if all the Juniper Berry Max Factor Lip Stay I had applied had worn off on my wine glass. I followed the bartender back to his makeshift bar, a foldout table my mother had covered with a linen tablecloth. He pulled a clipboard out of a carton and flipped a page. "I'm Caroline, by the way."

"Oh," he said, looking up. Good heavens his eyelashes were long. "I'm Anthony," he said. "I've been working at your mom's Christmas parties for years."

"Really?"

"Really," said Anthony. He held the clipboard toward me. "You can sign here."

"I never realized," I said, "that it was you."

"People don't."

"Oh," I said.

Anthony looked impatient. He poked the clipboard in my direction. "I have a question for you," I said.

"Do you?" said Anthony. "What's that?"

"How do you know how much to bring?"

"How much liquor?"

"Yeah, and wine."

He smiled. "My dad's been doing the same parties for a long time," he said. "You know who's going to be where." He nodded to the man in the bow tie. "He's going to drink vodka, and his wife used to like her gin. So you'd figure a half bottle for her. The Watsons, they drink wine. Mr. Kenton, Scotch. Mrs. Kenton, G&T's. You get the picture."

"And my mom?"

"Pinot grigio and soda," Anthony said, smiling.

I smiled back. "Me?"

"You don't live here anymore," said Anthony. "Your sister, though: pinot grigio, like your mom. But not tonight."

"What do you mean?"

"Well," said Anthony, "why don't you ask her?"

"Oh," I said. "I guess I will." After a pause, I said, "How about Ron?"

"Famous Grouse Scotch," said Anthony. He added quietly, "Like your dad."

"What?"

"Nothing. That was before my time, anyway."

I swallowed. "I like gin," I said, "and Scotch, sometimes. And beer."

"I like beer," said Anthony.

"Let me sign that," I said, taking the clipboard and signing my name under the enormous sum.

"Thanks."

"I live in New Orleans now," I said to Anthony, "and I'm a bartender, too. Well, cocktail waitress."

"I'm not a bartender," said Anthony. "I own the store."

"Oh."

"Your mom, she requests me. Tradition, I guess." We looked at my mother. She was beautiful, her smile lit from the glow of the tiny white lights she had strung around the branches of the Christmas tree. She sipped her drink, and then she laughed.

"Why'd you move all the way down South?" said Anthony.

"Oh God," I said, "I hate it here."

"What's New Orleans like?"

"I don't know," I said, flustered. I had not expected him to be interested. "It's hot," I said. Anthony waited. "It's wild," I said. "Like another country. Normal rules don't apply."

"What do you mean?"

"I met someone last week at Midas Mufflers," I said, "who was on crutches. I asked him what happened. He had been driving down a one-way street when someone smashed into him driving the wrong direction."

Anthony looked confused.

"Things like that happen in New Orleans. That's what I'm saying. And people drop things on the ground. Like, I think I've had enough of this sandwich. I'll just drop the rest on the sidewalk!"

"Good place for dogs, then," said Anthony.

"I guess so."

Anthony hoisted a carton. "Well, have a great

Christmas," he said, "Caroline."

"Thanks," I said. I walked him out, past the last few guests, the untouched cheese ball, the remains of the maple ham. We passed underneath the doorway where my mother had hopefully hung the mistletoe, but as I said, it was already gone.

FOUR

MADELINE WAS UP EARLY, drinking tea. By the time I shuffled downstairs in my pajama pants and T-shirt, she had cinnamon rolls in the oven. There was also a full pot of coffee, and I poured myself a cup. "Good morning, sleepyhead," said Madeline.

I smiled. "Is that the *Times?*"

"Yup." She pushed the paper toward me.

"You've been up a while?"

"I couldn't sleep."

I sipped my coffee. "Really?" I said. "You know what helps, a late-night Scotch."

She laughed. "I'll have to remember that."

It was strange, sitting at the breakfast table with my sister. There was so much between us. Our whole stories, up to a point, were the same. But when Ellie disappeared, my relationship with Madeline crumbled slowly. We stopped spending time in the imaginary city we had made in our backyard, stopped using the nicknames we had created for that place.

Madeline and I blamed each other, or reminded each other, or something.

When I was sixteen, I went away to boarding school in Connecticut, and Madeline stayed home. She wrote letters to me for a while, but when I didn't answer, she stopped. She kept sending birthday cards, though, every year. I tried to remember her birthday, but most years, I forgot. I knew her–there was almost no need for words–but I did not know who she had become. This new Madeline, someone's wife, someone who lived in New York City, a place I had always thought of as metal-gray and cold. I had never even seen her apartment.

"I have to talk to you about something," she said.

"Yes?"

"A few things, actually."

"Sounds bad," I said.

"Well," she said, "it's...."

"Ellie," I said. "I know." She was always between us. Ellie, who was gone.

"He's coming over today."

"Who?"

Madeline looked down at her wedding ring, twisted it. "Ken," she said, "the Simpsons' lawyer."

"You're on a first-name basis, huh?"

She looked up, anger flashing in her eyes. "That's not fair."

"And it's fair to forget her?" I said.

"I'm not...," Madeline sighed. "I'm trying to find some closure," she said.

"Yeah," I said. "That's what I hear." I stood, lifted my cup from the table.

"I'm sorry," said Madeline. "I know this is hard for you."

"It's hard for everyone," I said.

"He'll be here at one," said Madeline.

My mother was still asleep, and I stood in the doorway to her room. She looked so fragile in her wide, white bed. I remembered how she had gone to bed before my father every evening, leaving him drinking in the den.

I would come in to say goodnight to my mother and she would slide her reading glasses down her nose, look up from whatever British murder mystery she was reading, and open her arms to me.

I was right next to her, and suddenly I missed her so much my throat felt hot with tears. She opened her eyes. "Hi, cutie," she said. I smiled, clutching my coffee cup. My mom sat up in bed, reached her arms heavenward. "What a party!" she said. And then, her arms still open, she said, "Come here," and I did.

The lawyer was not a professional-looking man. He was, in fact, disheveled. I had expected a gray-haired fellow, distinguished in a Brooks Brothers suit. But when I wandered downstairs, I found my sister sitting on the couch next to a scrappy-looking dude in a leather jacket. Leather jacket! "Caroline," Madeline said, standing. Ron sat on a wing chair, looking a bit peaked.

I walked toward the unhappy threesome, held out my hand.

The lawyer stood and took it. "Ken Dowland," he said. I closed one eye. Had I seen him on late-night TV?

"Caroline Winters," I said. "Hi." He shook my hand, and I shook back. His fingers were cold, but then, it was December.

"Where's Mom?" said Madeline.

"She'll be down in a sec," I said. "Hear the hair dryer?"

"Oh," Madeline smiled, "yeah."

We exchanged pleasantries—*yes, all the wreaths seem to be up, no not too much salt on the roads, wouldn't it be great to have snow on Christmas?*—and then my mother came down the stairs, dressed in a sweater with reindeer on it. She wore matching red socks with loafers and corduroy pants. "Oh, hello!" she said gaily, as if the lawyer who wanted us to declare Ellie dead was a treasured guest.

"Hi," said Ken Dowland, rising again.

"Don't get up," said my mother, but she, too, shook his hand.

"Well," said Ken, "I guess Madeline's told you why I'm here."

There was no sound. "Ah," said Ken, "I'll backtrack." He rubbed his palms together. "I'll begin at, ah, the beginning."

"Would anyone like some hot cider?" asked my mother.

"I sure would," I said.

"Sure," said Ron amiably. Madeline shot him a look. "What?" he said.

"It'll just be a minute," said my mother, standing and heading toward the kitchen. "I'll put a cinnamon stick in each one!" she called.

*

Ken Dowland crossed his legs. His mug of cider hung precariously from one finger. "I'll begin at the beginning," he said. My mother's eyebrows were raised as if she was fascinated, but I could tell from her dull eyes that she wasn't listening. Madeline looked keyed up. Ron studied his fingernails, which I was unnerved to note had been manicured.

"In 1989, as I'm sure you know, Helen Simpson disappeared on her way home from Cedar Place School in Yonkers. She was eleven." Ken reached into his nylon backpack—what kind of lawyer carries a backpack?—and pulled out a dog-eared manila envelope. From it, he took three snapshots and placed them on the table. In one picture, Helen sat on the lap of a woman with a bad perm. Helen was cute: messy hair, the whole bit. She wore glasses and a green windbreaker. Ken didn't say anything as he laid out the pictures. The second picture showed Helen in a gauzy dress, blowing out candles on a birthday cake. The last picture was Helen by herself, looking embarrassed in a Halloween costume. I believe she was supposed to be a banana.

Ken Dowland cleared his throat. "Helen walked to and from school every day. On the morning of September twenty-fifth, she did not come home. Her mother," he pointed to the women with the bad perm, "called the police at five-oh-six p.m."

My mother began to cry, silent tears down her cheeks, but Ken pressed on. "A statewide search was conducted. Helen's coat," he pointed to the green windbreaker, "was found in a motel room along I-95. For ten years, there was no further trace of Helen Simpson." I was beginning to be pretty sure I had seen Ken Dowland on late-night television. He seemed the type.

"In 1999, a man named Leonard Christopher was arrested in upstate New York for the rape and murder of Allie Stephens." Ken whipped out the photo: another little girl, another heartbreaking smile, this one above a T-shirt that said, "A Chorus Line." My mother was crying full-on, now, and I was getting tired of Ken's dramatic act. I didn't like thinking of Ellie as nothing more than a blurry snapshot.

"Christopher led the police to a field in Syracuse," said Ken, "and showed them where he had buried Allie." He tapped the photo. "Allie's body was exhumed, and other bones were found near the site, teeth that were proven to be Helen Simpson's." Another tap. Madeline put her hand over her mouth.

"Look, Ken, let's cut to the chase here," said Ron, surprising everyone.

Ken nodded soberly. He gathered the photos and leaned toward my mother. "Leonard Christopher has told his cellmate there were other girls. Since Yonkers is only twenty miles from here, we decided to contact you when Leonard described a girl who sounds like your...," his voice trailed off, but just for a moment. "Like Ellie," he said, and then he continued. "Leonard Christopher's trial begins in February. His cellmate is willing to testify. In order to try him for your daughter's murder, however, Ellie needs to be declared dead, and not missing."

"Christ," said Ron, shaking his head.

"What if she's not dead?" said my mother. There was a hush in the living room, all the gaiety of the Christmas party gone. Ken stole a look at Madeline, who stood up.

"Thanks Ken," she said. "We'll be in touch."

Ken stood and shook her hand. "I really appreciate your time," he said, "and the, um, cider." He gestured to his drink, untouched on the coffee table, and leaving a wet ring that would be impossible to remove.

My mother stared into her lap. She wasn't crying anymore.

That night was Christmas Eve mass, and as usual, Ron and I were ready first. He sat in the den rubbing his eyes. He wore a navy-blue suit, and his tie had candy canes on it. He was freshly shaven, his wet hair combed back from his forehead. When I came down the stairs, he looked up and smiled. "Hey sis," he said.

"Hi," I said. "Are you still smoking?"

"No," said Ron, taking a pack from his jacket pocket and grinning wickedly.

We walked down by the water, our hands shoved in our pockets for warmth. "How's the Big Easy?" said Ron.

"Oh," I said, "Big. Easy."

"Lots of crazy times?"

I laughed. "Hardly."

"Did you buy Cisco when I told you to?"

"No, Ron," I said, "I didn't."

"Good thing."

We sat on the bench overlooking Long Island Sound. Behind us was the condo complex pool, emptied for the winter. "I've never even seen your apartment in the city, isn't that weird?" I said.

"Better hurry," said Ron.

"What does that mean?"

"We may be moving," said Ron, exhaling into the winter night.

"Where?"

Ron shook his head. "Ask your sister," he said.

We sat without speaking for a time. "You know," said Ron, finally, "Maddy misses her too. Just as much as you do."

"Of course," I said. I was not interested in getting into it with Ron. We had never seen eye-to-eye. After they became engaged, Madeline brought Ron to New Orleans to meet me. Ron looked at my apartment with such scorn that I almost punched him. "Imagine what you could do with this place if you *tried*," I heard him telling Madeline when he thought I was out of earshot. They stayed at the Ritz Carlton in the Quarter, and when I offered to take them on a tour of my favorite neighborhood bars, Ron declined quickly. At the end of the visit, he asked me if I needed money. I called him an asshole, and I wasn't sure if we'd moved past that.

"We all miss her," I said, trying to think of another topic that would get us back to the condo. World events? The economy of New Orleans? The new Saints stadium?

"The difference is," said Ron, standing up and throwing his cigarette into the water, "that Maddy thinks it's her fault."

"What?"

Ron smiled sadly. "Ask your sister," he said, again.

I looked at my cigarette, glowing between my fingers, and I brought it to my lips.

FIVE

I GAVE MADELINE HER FIRST CIGARETTE when she was thirteen. "Now, tap the pack," I said, demonstrating against the inside of my own wrist. She did as I told her, her forehead creased with concentration. Her white hair fell against her cheek. "Take one out," I said.

She looked up. "Which one?"

"Any one, nerd." From the floor, where she was sitting on her knees and turning the pages of Miss Nelson Is Missing, *Ellie giggled, and I saw the space where she had lost her first tooth. She was five, much younger than us. She should have been in bed, but could not sleep when the screaming began.*

Madeline took a cigarette from the pack (we were smoking Winston Lights, the brand James O'Hara smoked) and clamped it between her teeth. I took a match and held it underneath her cigarette until the paper caught. "Now breathe in, but just into your mouth," I said.

Madeline did as she was told, her eyes widening as the smoke burned her gums. She took the cigarette from her mouth, using all of her fingers in a fist. "Ow," she said, her voice wavering.

Ellie looked at me, fear like a flame behind her blue eyes. She was so fragile, not yet bruised. From downstairs, something slammed against a wall. My father's voice rumbled, and Ellie made a frightened sound.

"Oh, Jesus," I said, taking the cigarette from Madeline. I stubbed it out in a teacup, yanked the window open, and threw the cigarette. The wind smelled of rain and grass, and the clouds were swollen. The leaves outside were a vivid green. My parents were on the patio now, or the lawn. Something smashed against the side of the house, something glass. My mother: oh Joseph, Joseph! *Her voice thin and desperate.*

Madeline, looking down at the rug, her fingers snaking through the aqua plush. Ellie, hands pulled into fists, her breathing ragged as she willed herself not to cry.

It began to rain. A car driving by, the sizzling sound of tires on wet road. My father, his face red, his breath stinking of expensive Scotch. My mother, skinny as a skeleton in high-heeled sandals. Joseph, pleeease! *Her voice like steam, rising into nothing.*

We slept together in the closet that night. Madeline practiced smoking in front of the mirror, and became passably good, although I told her she couldn't inhale until her birthday. I showed her how to hold the cigarette between her first and second fingers, and explained how to exhale, how to make smoke rings. Ellie fell asleep on the floor before we did, curled around herself like a snail. Madeline and I changed into our pajamas and brushed our teeth in the bathroom. We were always listening for footfalls on the staircase: rapid running meant my mother in hysterics, and steady, creaking steps meant my father.

Even though we hid ourselves deep in my walk-in closet, I lay awake and waited, wanting to be ready. There had been nights when hours of peace gave way to the heavy footsteps coming up the stairs. The slurred and needling voice, Girls?

I stayed awake. I whispered my favorite word to my sisters to take their mind off things. "LaGuardia," I sang, "LaGuardia, LaGuardia, LaGuardia...." The name of our airport sounded like a creek bubbling slowly over stones. We chanted our homemade lullaby and fell into sleep, snuggled in Laura Ashley comforters. I listened to the rain outside our million-dollar house. The rain fell on my mother's Oldsmobile, on my father's company car, and on his Alfa Romeo. It fell on the garage downtown where James O'Hara worked, and on our treehouse in the woods. It fell on Holt, and New York City, and maybe even as far as New Orleans.

Wet streets. The smell of tar releasing heat. A morning, leaves against the kitchen window. My mother is asleep, her hair across the pillow, shut the door. My father, gone already to catch the train, his glass rinsed and waiting in the kitchen sink. Blue bowls laid out on the kitchen table with cold spoons beside them. A newspaper wrapped in plastic. Orange juice, the arrival of Mrs. Lake and the carpool. What a storm, hey girls? Wow—did you see the lightning? Maddy, your hair looks adorable!

I have checked: my sisters and I look perfect, hair and shoes and clothes as clean as if we had parents. Mrs. Lake backs down our driveway, gravel crunching under the tires, and for seven hours we are free.

*

Ellie looked like a normal five-year-old—wide-eyed, awkward—but she was courageous. "I wanna be a runaway," she said, after dinner one night, as we were watching Beverly Hills, 90210 *in Madeline's room. She put her hands on her hips. My mother and father were downstairs, but nothing had happened yet. Ellie pointed to the television. "None of them have parents," she said. On the screen, a blond girl drove a convertible to an ice cream shop, where her friends greeted her with great enthusiasm.*

"A runaway!" said Madeline, furrowing her brow. "Where did you even hear that word?"

Ellie pushed Mute on the remote control. Her face was animated. Madeline had pulled Ellie's hair into pigtails, and they stuck out above her ears. "We can all be runaways," she said.

Madeline let out a nervous laugh. "Oh yeah, and where would we run to?" she said. She stopped painting her toenails.

"I wanna run away," said Ellie again. She said it slowly, gravely, and she looked into my eyes.

"OK," I said.

"Caroline," said Madeline, with barely disguised alarm, "We're just kids!"

Ellie smiled. That smile, the gap where a tooth had been. I dream of her, still: Ellie at that moment, before it all went wrong.

Madeline ran from the room, and from downstairs ice crashed into a crystal glass, and on the television a girl in a red sweater slapped a boy.

*

The idea of running away was just that—an idea—until James

O'Hara. I first noticed James the day I got my braces off. After the wrenching removal and Polaroid photo session (my picture was tacked up on a thumbtack board of perfect smiles, right between Arthur Waldenstein and Jenni Woods), I began to walk home. Though I had learned to drive the summer before, taking the Oldsmobile out into sparsely populated areas and making wide turns while my mother gave me directions, I wasn't yet legal.

My mother was at a Twig meeting, so I was supposed to take a cab back to Holt High School. I was wearing a denim miniskirt and the sun was out; I decided to walk instead.

I put one Treetorn in front of the other, a slight sway in my hips that I had never felt quite able to pull off before, when I had a mouth full of metal. Suddenly, there was nothing standing between me and adulthood, I thought. I had gotten what I needed from my parents (I knew that orthodontia and piano lessons were expensive) and could now move forward in the world.

I passed Mimi's Café, Stride-Rite, and Baskin-Robbins. I passed the deli where my sisters and I had bought a 12-pack of Jolt Cola and drank it in an hour, spinning and reeling from the thrill of it, running barefoot across the lawn and feeling the breeze in our hair before the nausea took hold and we had to go inside and tell our mother we were sick. I passed the Liquor Barn.

And then there was Ray's Fuel, the local gas station and body shop. We stopped at Ray's all the time, when my mother needed the car filled (I didn't know until I went away that you could pump gas yourself; Holt has no self-serve pumps). I had never really looked inside the body shop. It seemed a secret place, full of oily-smelling things that wouldn't make sense to me.

I suppose I had never thought about who worked there, or anywhere, for that matter. All I knew of work was my father with his briefcase and his bitter smell, the way his mouth tightened when he had to write a check for anything. My father worked on Wall Street, in New York City. People gave him money, and he invested it for them. Sometimes he made lots of money, like the time he bought my mother some land on Martha's Vineyard. But sometimes he lost money, like the year afterward, when he had to sell the land and my mother had to sell her family's house in Savannah, too.

My father gave my mother an allowance, and if I needed anything, I had to write a proposal, outlining what amount of money I needed and why, and he would decide if it was worthwhile. Five dollars for the spring formal was not worthwhile, so I stole the money from my mother's Gucci purse.

I was fifteen with straight teeth and a denim miniskirt and I looked inside that dusky place behind Ray's Fuel, and I saw James O'Hara.

I know now that a boy in oil-stained coveralls looking for love is a cliché, but the sweet shock James sent through me was like a drug. He was cleaning a wrench with a red cloth, and he turned around as I walked by. He smiled in a shy way and I didn't just smile back, I stopped.

"Hey," said James O'Hara, and I said, "Hey."

I didn't see him again for another few months, but I asked around about him. I did not have many friends—my sisters and I tended to spend our time together—but I was able to glean that the new mechanic at Ray's Fuel was named James and was an orphan. He was supposed to be a senior at Holt High School, but

I never saw him there. Maybe he was a dropout.

I developed a full-blown obsession. I explained to my mother I wanted to walk home every day. Her distracted driving was enough of a reason, but I told her that I was training for a March of Dimes Walk-A-Thon. Relieved, I think, she told me to take my sisters with me. We could use the exercise, she said, and she would have more time to write in her journal. "I have stories, you know," she told me, raising her eyebrows and holding my gaze until I felt uncomfortable.

I didn't say that I had already heard all her stories: the one about her rich fiancé Bernard, the one about her aborted modeling career. I was sick to death of her stories. They all ended the same way: a depressed woman sitting alone in an expensive kitchen.

My sisters fell in love with James O'Hara, too. We knew about the orphanage in White Plains (there were dances at the yacht clubs to benefit the orphanage, and bake sales), but we had never met a real orphan before. To me, it seemed romantic to be alone in the world, with no parents making you miserable. We stopped every day to get bags of Gummi bears or Cokes from the snack shop at Ray's Fuel, and sometimes James came out of the garage and we'd see him. He always smiled at me, and once even asked my name. I felt as if he watched me while I picked out candy or a soda. He watched me in a way that was new to me, a way that made me feel powerful.

Madeline pronounced him cuter than Kirk Cameron.

A long time went by with things just like this: Skittles and Twizzlers and Gummi bears and Jolt Cola and hoping for a glance of the orphan. Things at home were both boring and ter-

rifying. Days would go by slowly, the air in our house sour with the sadness of a dying marriage. But then an argument would ignite my father's anger, and we would try to hide in the backyard or my closet until the tornado of his frustrated hopes had passed.

Later, I wondered who my father might have been without the alcohol in his blood. He had swept my mother off her feet, charmed her with his intellect and rugged looks. I knew this because she had told me, and yet it was hard to believe. Sometimes, I caught him gazing at me as if I was a beautiful object he had forgotten he owned.

But more often, he was angry. We never knew what might set him off, so we hated inviting anyone to our house. After Ellie went to kindergarten and my mother let the nanny go, my sisters and I were alone.

And then James called.

"Hello?" said my mother, one sunny Saturday. Saturdays (and Sundays, for that matter) filled me with dread. So much could go wrong. I usually spent the day practicing, hoping that if I filled the house with piano notes, there would be less room for yelling. I tried to lose myself in the music, tried to fill the corners with light.

This Saturday, my father was mowing the lawn, having had a glass of wine for breakfast. My mother had put on her tennis skirt and visor with the pretense of going somewhere and doing something, but then fought with my father about the wine and lost her steam. Slowly, my father's volatile personality had alienated her from her friends, and now she rarely made plans at all. She was sitting at the kitchen table staring into space when the phone rang.

"Oh," said my mother, putting her palm over the phone and turning to me. "For you. A boy," she whispered, raising her eyebrow and winking lasciviously. Her thighs, underneath her tennis skirt, were bony and gray. She had fixed her hair carefully, curls tumbling over the visor like a waterfall.

I was playing Colecovision with Ellie, Donkey Kong. *I took the phone, my heart thumping. "Hello?" I said.*

"Is this Caroline?" said a voice that was low and adult.

"Yes."

"This is James, um, from Ray's Gas Mart?"

"Yes?" My first thought was that it was a joke, but I held the phone to my ear and looked at the kitchen floor: stripped pine.

"I was wondering?" There was a pause, and I heard someone talking in the background, the clang of metal. A vision of James came to me: his thick eyebrows and heavy-lidded eyes. The smell of car exhaust and oil. His hands holding something heavy, a tool, the murky light of the shop with only a dirty window to let Saturday in. The pay phone on the wall, and James' black boots with the band of leather around the ankle fastened by a tarnished buckle.

My mother was staring at me, opening her palms, mouthing who is it, *her face glowing.*

"Yes?" I said into the phone.

"Would you...like to go out for some pizza? With me?"

"Yes," I said. Warmth filled me—I could actually feel my veins expanding.

"How about next Wednesday at, um, six?"

"Yes." I hung up the phone, and my mother said, "Well?

What is it?"

Ellie was still playing Donkey Kong, *her thumb hitting the red button and making her little man jump, but I knew she was listening. I could have turned to my mother and told her about the boy. Boys were something she loved to talk about, her old loves, her glory days. But I did not confide in my mother. It was too late by then.*

"Nothing," I said, and I went outside to sit in the hammock and savor my secret like a hoarded Godiva chocolate. Madeline was in the hammock already, reading a Nancy Drew, and Ellie soon joined us.

Behind the hammock was an expanse of wooded land. We had made a secret world there, one filled not with trees but with chic apartments and restaurants where we went on dates. Madeline, who was called Moo, had a job as a teacher and a boyfriend named Renaldo. Ellie, who called herself Laurel, was a busy actress. And I, as Candy, had a career as a famous musician. (In the real world, I took piano lessons three times a week.) James O'Hara had been my imaginary boyfriend for months; now I had a real date to plan for.

We spent many afternoons in our made-up city, stopping into each other's apartments and discussing our boyfriends and careers. Even in our imaginations, my sisters and I played our roles. Madeline was the good one: she did imaginary laundry. Ellie dove headlong into pretend adventures, like sailing in the hammock to Tahiti.

I kept us safe. It was my job in our real lives and our dreams, and I took it seriously. I didn't trust anyone, and I was always ready for something to go wrong. Sometimes I wonder who I would have been if I hadn't had sisters. Maybe I would have been the good one. Maybe I would have been able to take a chance.

I do not know what my mother did that Saturday; when we came inside for dinner (we made peanut butter and bologna sandwiches for ourselves), she was still sitting at the kitchen table in her ridiculous tennis getup, looking out at nothing.

We did not feel sorry for them, my parents, wandering miserably through their grand house like ghosts. All we knew was that they were not like other parents, and we hated them for it. Other mothers spent afternoons making a cake with you, not sleeping or talking about their old boyfriends. Other fathers sat down to dinner, and played Zim Zam on Sunday afternoons instead of drinking in the den. When you are small, if you reach out, and nobody takes your hand, you stop reaching out, and reach inside, instead. That's just the way it was.

The night of my date with James O'Hara was damp. It was March, and the weather was unpredictable. With my sisters, I chose an outfit carefully: denim miniskirt, pantyhose, green and yellow striped sweater with a plain white T-shirt underneath, in case the restaurant was overheated. I told my sisters I wouldn't kiss James O'Hara, but secretly considered it.

My parents didn't usually care where we went at night. Sometimes, we walked to the library or, in the summer, to the Cherokee Golf Club. A mother took us all bowling or to Pizza Hut once in a while. It was never our mother.

I did not tell my parents that I had a date on Wednesday.

Somehow, I thought it would all work out.

James rang the bell at precisely six. I was ready to go: I smelled of my mother's Chanel No. 5, and my socks were bunched just right above my sneakers. My father was in the den, the door closed, the sound of Benny Hill behind it. My mother was in the back of the house or in bed, I didn't care. My sisters and I sat cross-legged in the front hallway waiting. We generally avoided the front hallway, as it was too close to my father's den; the door could swing open suddenly, say, if my father wanted another drink, and there you'd be: caught, and he could tell you you were fat or lazy or he would want to wrestle on the rug.

Madeline's eyes widened when the bell rang. Ellie's face bloomed with her grin. I stood, never feeling more like a queen than at that moment, but before I could take a step, the door to the den opened. Madeline made a panicked sound. My father appeared in a bathrobe. His eyes were bleary, full of both confusion and cruelty.

The bell rang again. "Who is it?" my father asked. By now, my mother had come into the front hallway as well.

"How am I supposed to know?" I said.

My father pulled his bathrobe closed, yanked the sash around his fat stomach (the alcohol was causing his girth to widen, although I did not know this at the time). He opened the door.

Standing on our front steps, James looked like an angel. He wore a nylon jacket, jeans, and a navy sweater. From five feet away, I smelled his cologne: Drakkar Noir. He had shaven, but I could see where the hair had been.

I cannot remember if I actually felt lust at that moment, or if I even knew what lust was, or if I just wanted to be owned by someone other than my parents. James looked at me, and the room fell away.

"Can I help you?" said my father.

"Oh," said my mother, "it's the boy from the body shop."

"I'm James," said James, and he brought a bunch of carnations forward. Their stems had been wrapped carefully with aluminum foil. "I'm here for Caroline," he said.

"Oh, you're here for Caroline, are you?" said my father, his eyes narrowing.

"Yes, sir," said James.

"Well, well, well," said my father. He put his hands on his hips, and I could see him trying to decide how to handle the situation. "Why don't you give me just a second to have a word with my wife?" he said, finally. My mother followed my father back into his den.

James was still standing in the hallway. He looked puzzled and a little frightened.

"I'm Ellie," said my baby sister, holding up her hand in a wave. She was not quite as tall as James' chest, and he bent down to her.

"I know you," said James. Ellie's cheeks grew pink. She was wearing leggings and a T-shirt with bare feet, and her hair had not been cut in a long time. It fell in snarls and split ends down her back. Ellie's eyes danced, and she drew her palms together and grinned.

"And don't I know you, too?" said James to Madeline, who nodded, speechless.

"That's Madeline," said Ellie.

"Hello, Madeline," said James.

Madeline did not speak.

The door to the den opened, and my father came out with an arm tightly around my mother. My father's fingers on her shoulder were red.

"James, is it?" said my father.

"Yes, sir."

"James, my wife and I have had a little talk," said my father, and my mother tried to meet my eyes. I knew what was coming; I looked down. "You won't be taking Caroline anywhere," said my father. "Good night."

"Oh," said James, and my father led him out by the elbow and shut the door in his face.

"Well then," he said, "I'm ready for a little fresher-upper."

I turned to him. "Fuck you," I said. There was a pause, and then he lifted his hand and brought his palm to my cheekbone. We stood across from each other for a long moment, my face hot. My father struck me again, my sisters silent, and my mother stood and watched.

We planned our escape carefully. We decided that the Oldsmobile made the best getaway car: the company car and the BMW were too flashy, but no one would notice an Oldsmobile. We could live in it, too, if necessary.

We had some money. I babysat for years, and was a Junior Lifeguard at the Oyster Shores Club. I had saved about three hundred dollars. Madeline kept everything that was given to her—each birthday card with ten dollars, each letter from our grandfather with money—and she had put away about two hundred dollars. There was an American Express card for emer-

gencies, but using it, of course, would give us away. We made a trip to the Holt Pharmacy, where we stocked up on gum and hair spray. Madeline, ever the pragmatist, bought a bottle of cough medicine, bags of nature trail mix, and sunscreen.

Ellie didn't have any material possessions, of course, but what she had was precious: a belief that life had joy in store for us, and an unwavering faith in me.

We spent evenings, in those final weeks at home, hunched over the Rand McNally Atlas, trying to decide where to spend the rest of our lives. The Atlas made me want to cry: it was a wedding present to my parents from someone who had written "For all the adventures you'll share!" My father hated to travel, and after their disastrous honeymoon on Sea Island, my parents hadn't really gone anywhere except Savannah.

Looking back, I think we chose New Orleans because it was what Madeline wanted. Madeline was unsure from the start about the whole plan, and we wanted her to be happy. When we watched A Streetcar Named Desire *on television, late one night, Madeline was rapt. "Could we go there?" she said, and we said yes.*

New Orleans seemed like the perfect place: dreamy and warm. We imagined everyone there was blond, and dressed in silk. We loved Baskin-Robbins daiquiri ice cream, and assumed it would be even better down south. Our mother was from the South, and we had all heard stories about how wonderful it was, how beautiful her life had been before she had gone and married a Yankee.

*

cided to wait until the last day of school, June seventeenth. n the night of the sixteenth, we packed the car, knowing that my mother never drove it anymore. She rarely even got out of bed. I almost wished we could bring her, but she wasn't strong enough to make it, and we were. She'd probably call my father from the pay phone at some McDonald's, begging to come back home. I hated her.

"Colecovision?" said Ellie.

"No!" I said. "We might not even have a TV."

Ellie's face sobered as she tried to contemplate such a thing.

"I'm bringing all the Lord of the Rings *books," said Madeline.*

"OK," I said. "And clothes. We might have to get jobs, so bring some nice stuff."

"Jobs?" said Ellie.

"Not you, probably," I admitted.

"Gummi bears?" said Ellie.

"Sure," I said. "Bring all the candy you want."

It was strange to pack up our rooms. We had to leave so much behind, but we had things we didn't need, or even want, when it came down to it. I wanted all of my hair stuff, I'm embarrassed to say, and my self-tanning cream and pink razor. There was a part of me that believed looking beautiful was the source of all happiness. My mother had told us as much, every time she started to ramble and elaborate on what a beauty she had once been. And it was true, she had been lovely. She kept a scrapbook of all her magazine ads (she had pages from Vogue, Mademoiselle, *and* McCalls'*), and in the pictures she looked as if everything was in front of her. Her smile was real. But look* *what had happened to her.*

"Don't forget sleeping bags," I told my sisters, "and toothbrushes." Madeline packed carefully, folding everything and pressing out wrinkles, while Ellie just crammed it all in. When our bags and pillowcases were filled, we snuck down to the garage where the car was parked. We knew how to walk carefully on the stairs. Our mother was in bed, the lights turned off, but our father was in his den.

The only sounds in the house were the muffled television and my sisters' breathing. It was thirty-six steps to the bottom.

The garage was cool and damp. We didn't turn on the lights, just felt our way along the cement wall. We could see the dim outline of the cars. "Don't open the car door," whispered Ellie. "He'll hear it." Her cotton nightgown fell to her toes. She smelled of Pert Plus shampoo.

"Where should we put them?" asked Ellie. Her pillowcase was filled to bulging, and she could barely hold it in her chubby arms.

"Under the car," I said. "I'll get them in the morning."

We had just stashed everything when we heard footsteps. "Yikes!" said Madeline.

We looked for a place to hide, and then the door that led from the house into the garage opened.

"Hello?" said our father, "who's there?"

We stood silent, waiting for his eyes to adjust to the shadowy light, waiting for him to see us.

SIX

"CAROLINE?" It was Ron, his hand on my shoulder. "You ready to go back to the condo? Don't want to miss Christmas mass."

I looked at Ron. He was smiling, and I saw that he hated all this as much as I did.

"Were you brought up with any religion?" I asked Ron, throwing my cigarette into the water and turning to walk back.

"My mom was a lapsed Episcopalian, but she took us to church once in a while," he said.

"Really? I thought the Catholic wedding was your deal."

"Mine? No. Maddy insisted on it."

"That surprises me," I said.

"Why?"

"I guess I didn't know she cared about things like that."

"You don't have any idea what she cares about," said Ron in a sharp voice.

Tears sprang to my eyes. "What's that supposed to mean?" I said.

"Forget it."

"I will," I said. I tried to swallow the anger I often felt around Ron and his judgment. We walked back to the house, and I could smell the ocean.

My mother and Madeline were standing outside the front door shivering. "Where have you *been*?" said my mother. She wore large, gold earrings.

"Just taking in Christmas Eve," said Ron, slipping his arm around Madeline, who seemed unresponsive. She had blown her hair straight, and wore a plaid headband that matched her shoes. She was engulfed in a mink coat.

"Nice coat!" I said.

"Anniversary," said Madeline, climbing into my mother's Mercedes.

Ron and Madeline's anniversary was in June, which seemed a strange time to give someone a mink coat. They had been married three years before. Ron started the Mercedes and my mother glanced at the car clock.

"Yeek," she said. "We're going to miss the carols!" She turned on the radio, and found a station playing "O Little Town of Bethlehem." "It's Elvis!" she said, delighted.

We drove past the gatehouse, waving to Mitchell, the senile man who protected us from whatever nefarious types lurked around a small Westchester town on Christmas Eve. "Have you been smoking?" Madeline whispered, disgustedly, to me.

"Yes," I said.

"God," said Madeline. She rolled down her window.

"Madeline," said my mother, "it's freezing. Roll that back up immediately."

Madeline sighed, but did as she was told.

At St. David's, we parked and walked quickly to the entrance. My mother was right: we had almost missed the carols. Nonetheless, she was able to walk up the aisle toward a pew, winking and smiling at her friends.

As soon as we genuflected and sat down, she began to fill me in on the year's gossip. As the mass wore on, my mother's voice in my ear was a comforting hum: *now see that woman with the bad haircut? That's the sister of Mary Lou, whose daughter's in rehab somewhere like St. Louis. Mary Lou was married to Owen—remember him? He bought twenty boxes of your Girl Scout cookies one year—but then his secretary got pregnant, at least Mary Lou got the house, that white colonial on Kenny Avenue, and her son's at Lawrenceville....*

I scanned the churchgoers for familiar faces, and saw a few: girls I'd known, now wearing blouses with big collars, children in their laps or by their sides. The church was decorated with dozens of poinsettia plants and white candles. When the priest passed the collection basket, Ron pulled a fifty from his wallet. Madeline gave him a look I didn't understand: a look between annoyance and pride. My mother pressed a quarter into my palm, the way she had done when I was small. I thought about protesting, pulling bills from my own purse (it was purple velvet; Winnie had given it to me for my birthday), but I kept quiet and dropped the quarter in the basket when it came by.

Right about Eucharist time, Madeline put her fingertips over her mouth. "Are you OK?" I whispered.

"No," she answered.

People were starting to shuffle in their seats, getting ready to receive the Lord and show off their Christmas outfits. "What's the matter?" I asked, but Madeline shook her head.

"Look," said my mother, nodding toward the line of people filing past our pew toward the altar. "Is that the ugliest dress you've ever seen or *what*?"

When the man in the gray suit stopped next to our pew, we stood and made our way toward the altar. As we passed people who had taken communion, my mother winked and smiled. I felt like a fraud taking the bread and wine, but didn't know what to say to get out of it. Madeline went before me, settling on her knees awkwardly and refusing the wine. She bent her head for a quick prayer—we knew that any prayers made at the altar were that much closer to God—and I looked at the back of her neck, exposed as her hair fell in two wings over her shoulders. The skin was pale.

I knelt, but realized I had forgotten which hand went on top to receive the bread, so I hurriedly stuck out my tongue. The priest murmured something and I murmured something back. He placed the wafer on my tongue. It was dry, and stuck to the roof of my mouth as I chewed. I closed my eyes and then I saw her: Ellie. She was kneeling at the altar, five years old and balling her fists, saying, "This is so boring!"

I opened my eyes, and a woman wearing too much base makeup was standing above me with the chalice. She had finished wiping the glass, and held it toward me. I brought the silver cup to my mouth and drank.

I'm alive, said Ellie.

I heard the voice. But then it was time for me to stand,

straighten my skirt, and follow Ron's wide back to the pew. I felt dizzy, but it had always been Ellie who had grown dizzy in church. She had once passed out, and my mother carried her outside and put her in the cool car with a soda from the machine in the rectory.

I knelt in our pew, and spoke to God. *God bless my father in heaven, and my mother. God bless Madeline and Ron. God bless Winnie and Jimbo and Georgette. God bless Ellie.*

I remembered the last time I had seen her, walking from Mrs. Lake's car into Maxwell Elementary. Her legs pumping, the sunlight making her brown hair shimmer. Her red T-shirt, her blue jeans and sneakers. Arms swinging at her sides.

As the choir began to sing around me, I pressed my eyes closed, to keep the tears inside. The organ rang out, the voices sang *Glooooria!* My mother pulled me to my feet and kissed my cheek. "Merry Christmas," she said.

Ellie had not looked back, that June morning. She just walked into her school, stepped inside, and the door closed behind her.

SEVEN

from the desk of

AGNES FOWLER

Dear Thomas,

I very much enjoyed my hot bath this evening–thanks to you! It makes me happy to know that the gas leak is completely repaired. And I loved chatting. It was nice to take a day off from work, though the banging around did give me a bit of a headache, and it's going to take me years to pay for the pleasure of your company. Just kidding! But I sure wish the library paid $75 an hour.

In any case, it was so interesting to hear about the many ways in which gas lines can spring leaks. I had no idea how complicated the pipes underneath the city were. And the story about the tunnels that run from City Hall to the Wilma Building...well, wow. Do you really think people smoked opium down there? I went on the web today at work, but I couldn't find any mention of this. I searched under "opium" and "Missoula," and although I did find the creepy web page of a young man who, in his own words, "sells the Wackiest Weed in the West," I did not find any historical documents. Perhaps I will try OCLC or the WLN databases tomorrow. Though I don't know how I would explain an extensive search for opium to my supervisor, Frances.

Can you tell I love my work? This is my second job. During college, I worked at the Orange Julius in the mall for three weeks, and I can make a mean sherbet smoothie. I lived at home, and my father told me I couldn't get a job. When he found my paper hat the jig was up. But he passed away recently, and I graduated from UMT with honors, so it seemed the time was ripe to pursue career opportunities.

I could have gone back to the Orange Julius at the mall, even though it was pretty embarrassing when my father dragged me out of there. Eventually, I have no doubt that I would have been Assistant Manager (or even Manager, someday!) but I felt I was meant to be something more. When the job opened up at the library, well, it seemed like fate. My supervisor, Frances, said I seemed "easygoing" and "moldable" from the start. I reminded her of herself, Frances said, when she was young and impressionable. I was hired and given an ID badge. I am proud to be a librarian.

I really do love a good research challenge. In this, Thomas, I think that maybe we are alike. Finding and organizing information is much like finding a gas leak and repairing it. It's all about order…taking the strange twists and turns of life (or gas!), the bits of experience and memory (or gas!), and making them into a straight line. Sealing off the leaks, so to speak.

Well, I am going on. I just wanted to say thank you, and I very much enjoyed our time together. I'm at the library (InterLibrary Loan Office, also known as "ILL") all day, if you'd like to say hello. And I'm going to be around all weekend. If you feel like a glass of wine or some coffee cake, do stop by! (You know where I live.)

All best,
Agnes Fowler

EIGHT

"I WONDER if Santa Claus will come," said my mother in the car on the way home from mass. We were sharing the backseat, as if Madeline and Ron were our parents. Nobody answered my mother. I wished I were back in New Orleans, sitting with Winnie at the Napoleon House, drinking a Pabst Blue Ribbon.

"I feel sick," said Madeline.

"Oh, sweetie," said Ron, touching her leg. I thought about Anthony from the Liquor Barn. Did he have to work on Christmas Eve?

"Can we stop and get a bottle of wine?" I asked.

"We have plenty of wine at home," said my mother.

"Oh," I said.

"And I have the ornaments ready," she said.

"Great," said Ron. My mother smiled. Every year, she gave us each an ornament on Christmas Eve, and a nightgown. (Ron got pajamas.) We listened to Cole Porter or Elvis Christmas records, and drank. It was awful. I wondered if I could get a late-night flight back to my little apartment on Esplanade. In the morning, Winnie's kids would open their presents, and her common-law husband, Kit, would fry a turkey in an enormous vat of oil. Winnie would make crawfish stuffing.

"Are you OK?" said Madeline. She had turned around to look at me.

"What?"

"You look like you're about to cry," said Madeline. She sought my gaze.

"I think you look great, sweetie," said my mother. "No matter what anyone says about your pants being tight."

"Who said anything about my pants being tight?"

"Nobody, honey!" said my mother. "Little Miss Sensitive," she said to Madeline. I wanted to scream, but did not. Finally, we turned into the condo complex. Ron honked the horn, waking Mitchell.

"Merry Christmas, Mitchell," said Ron.

"Well," said Mitchell, "and the same to you."

Ron waited patiently for a minute, and then said, "Could you open the gate for us, Mitchell?"

"Oh, my, yes, of course." Mitchell hit the button, and we drove inside.

"Maybe I shouldn't have given him twenty dollars for Christmas," said my mother thoughtfully.

I was in the bedroom, trying to get a look at my bottom in the mirror, when Madeline came rushing in. "Have I gained weight?" I said. "Are my pants tight?"

"Jesus!" said Madeline. She went into the bathroom and closed the door, turning on the faucet.

"Girls! Time for ornaments!" called my mother from downstairs.

Madeline came out of the bathroom, her lips pressed together. "This is excruciating," I said. "I can't bear it. I want to go home."

"Oh, Caroline," said Madeline, "your life is not that bad. Open the ornament, how hard is that?"

"For your information, I have friends in New Orleans who are missing me," I said.

"I'm sure you do," said Madeline.

"What is that supposed to mean?" I said.

"Anyone who hangs out in a bar," said Madeline, "will have friends eventually."

I sat still on the bed.

"I'm sorry," said Madeline.

"No," I said, "it's OK."

"It isn't," said Madeline. She sat down next to me. "I don't know what's wrong with me," she said.

"You're pregnant, seems to me," I said.

Madeline smiled wanly. "Due in April."

"That's so wonderful," I said.

"But there's something else. Ron's probably going to lose his job."

"Oh my God."

"It's not his fault."

"Madeline, of course not."

"I don't know what we're going to do." She sighed. "So

you see, sometimes I wish I worked in a bar," said Madeline. "I wish…lots of things."

I didn't say anything. As usual, my sister wanted something from me that I did not know how to give. My mother kept calling from downstairs.

"Why are you pushing this thing with Ken Dowland?" I said.

Madeline looked at her hands. Her fingernails, once her pride and joy, were bitten to the quick. "There are only so many questions one person can have in their life," she said.

"Are you sure, though?"

"Oh, Care," said my sister, "come on. We both know she's dead."

"I'm not sure," I said. "There's some part of me that feels her alive. I hear her voice."

"That's hope, not Ellie," said Madeline. "Go to therapy, they'll explain it to you."

"But what if it *is* Ellie?"

Madeline turned to me, her tired eyes, her cheekbones, her smell. "If it were Ellie," said Madeline, "if she were alive, why wouldn't I hear her, too? Because I don't hear her. I don't hear anything."

"There you are," said my mother, holding a spritzer. "Ron and I have been waiting by the Christmas tree!"

We went downstairs then, my sister and I, and we opened our ornaments. Mine was a seahorse made of blown glass, and Madeline had an angel with wild blond curls. Ron's ornament was a snowman wearing a top hat. We hung them on the tree, and then Madeline and I opened our holly-strewn nightgowns and Ron exclaimed over his pajamas, which were printed with tiny gifts and the words CHECK OUT MY PACKAGE! Later, after a few whiskeys, Ron said, "Do you think your mother has any idea what *package* means?" I looked at my mother, sipping wine and gaily turning the pages of an old baby album.

"I hope not," I said.

That night, as I lay in bed, I heard Madeline crying quietly. Instead of going to her, I pretended to be asleep. I promised myself, for the hundredth time, that this was without a shadow of a doubt my very last Christmas at home.

NINE

from the desk of

AGNES FOWLER

Dear Thomas,

What a thrill to meet your lovely family this weekend at the farmers' market. Your baby is just so cute, and your wife was very kind to mention the cookies I left for you at the front desk of Superman Plumbing. I do hope you were able to use all those beets she bought. What a hilarious story about losing your wedding ring down the Stenmeyers' drain! It still makes me chuckle. Enclosed please find the payment for the work on my gas line. (Still enjoying my hot water!)

My best to your wife and son,
Agnes Fowler

TEN

AS IF RESIGNED to the fact that I would never find a man and settle down, my family gave me wedding gifts for Christmas: a Cuisinart from Madeline and Ron, a blender and a set of knives from my mother. My aunt Rosalie (my father's sister) sent a gorgeous vase for Madeline and Ron, a box of chocolates for my mother, and a book for me: *Cooking for One.* I held it up. "This is just mean," I said, and my mother said, "No, honey! It's a compliment. Rosalie *wishes* she could have dinner without Uncle Lou."

We always spent Christmas Day with my mother's sister and her family. Following in my mother's footsteps, Blanche had married a Yankee and moved to New York. Uncle Wallace was a travel agent of sorts, although he worked only for very wealthy clients and preferred to be called a "consultant." My mother's sister hated to travel, and had made remaining a Southern belle her life's work. Blanche's accent had grown stronger every year she had lived in New York, and she routinely startled dinner guests with recipes from her Savannah Junior League cookbook: Shrimp Dip Divine; Frog Legs Geechee; Low Country Stuffed Mushrooms. She drank sherry and wore big floppy hats, as if headed to the beach. Her father had met Flannery O'Connor once, and this fact was dropped into many conversations.

As if to spite their mother, Remshart and Daisy had grown up with Brooklyn accents and fast-paced speech that required careful attention. Remshart was now sixteen, and wore Fubu and Sean John clothing, emulating the other rich white boys at his private school who dressed like rappers. Daisy was a slutty and difficult eighteen-year-old. I couldn't wait to see them.

As we were getting ready to head into the city, the phone rang. I answered, and Mitchell at the gate told me there was a delivery. Did Mitchell live in the gatehouse? I told him to send the deliveryman in, and answered the door a moment later. A man in a turtleneck sweater stood on my mother's welcome mat, holding a bottle wrapped in red paper. "Sign here," said the man, and I did.

My mother was fixing her hair. "Look," I said. She turned off the hair dryer and read the card. "It's from Anthony at the Liquor Barn," she said. "How sweet. He's never sent anything before." She unwrapped the bottle–it was champagne–and said, "Oh, goody. Put it in the fridge, will you?"

I brought the bottle downstairs, feeling giddy with pleasure. Ron was reading the paper at the kitchen table. "Look, champagne," I said.

"What?"

"The Liquor Barn sent it," I said.

"Wasn't that nice?" said Ron. He looked at me steadily. I poured another cup of coffee.

"What?" I said.

"I saw you flirting with that bartender at the party," said Ron.

"I don't know what you're talking about," I said. As I stowed away the bottle, the air from the refrigerator was cool on my face.

"Ho, ho, ho!" cried Uncle Wallace as hc opened his apartment door.

"Merry Christmas," I said, offering my cheek for a kiss. Uncle Wallace ignored it, planting a wet one on my mouth and then turning to Madeline. I made my way into the apartment, where Remshart, dressed in baggy jeans with a sideways baseball cap and a towel around his shoulders, was talking furtively into a cell phone. "Hi, Remy," I said, and he put his hand over the phone and said, "Yo, cuz."

"*Caroline!*" It was Aunt Blanche, rushing from the kitchen in a long dress. Her hair was styled carefully into a wave, and her skin was powdered. She pulled me toward her, and I smelled her Chantilly Lace perfume. "My darling girl," said Blanche, "you are truly more lovely every time I see you." I had worn a skirt, so that my mother couldn't make any further comments about tight pants.

"Thanks, Aunt Blanche," I said.

"Would you care for some lemonade?"

"Sure," I said, "I'd love some."

*

Daisy arrived about halfway through the shrimp dip. She looked sweaty and thin. “Daisy,” said Aunt Blanche, “will you look who’s here?”

Daisy slumped against the doorframe, her arms crossed over her peasant blouse. She had circles under her eyes. “Daisy was up late at a *gig*,” explained Aunt Blanche, using her forefingers to put quotation marks around the word “gig.”

Daisy stared at her mother.

“Daisy, sweetie, tell them about your *jam band*,” said Blanche, crunching her fingers in the air again.

“Lord help us,” said Uncle Wallace, “Now, Ron, how about a hot stock tip?”

“Oh, well,” said Ron, “I don’t know, Wallace.”

“*Madeline has news!*” screeched my mother.

“Mom,” said Madeline, holding her hands up, as if she could keep the words inside my mother.

“Is that right?” said Aunt Blanche, relieved to have the spotlight off Daisy, who wandered off to her room and began to blare “Sugar Magnolia.”

“Remshart, honey! Get off the phone, you rascal,” said Aunt Blanche. “Come in here for some news.”

“No,” said Madeline, “Really, there’s no news....” She glared at my mother. “Mom, we agreed,” she said.

Remshart swaggered into the room, his hands on his hips. “Whassup?” he said.

“Well?” said my mother, her eyes shining.

“Take that towel off your shoulders, dear,” said Aunt Blanche.

"No," said Remshart.

"Don't you speak to your mother that way," said Uncle Wallace, his face reddening.

"Chill," said Remshart.

"Why you–" said Uncle Wallace.

"Maddy? Honey?" said my mother.

"I think they call the towel a *do rag*," said Blanche. "The blacks, I mean."

Uncle Wallace reached for his son; Daisy, named for the sweet Southern belle of Fitzgerald's dreams, reached the decision that she would drop out of school to follow Phish; Aunt Blanche reached for her cigarettes; my mother reached the end of her rope. And then he came back from the kitchen, the savior of Christmas, my brother-in-law, Ron.

"I have an announcement," he said, holding the bottle of champagne from the Liquor Barn high. "We're going to have a baby!" he said, and then he popped the cork.

Over dinner, everyone toasted Madeline's new baby. Even Remshart seemed excited. Daisy, who ate a few green beans and then went back to her room, suggested Madeline should name her baby Forbin. Madeline smiled politely. She looked relieved to have the news of her pregnancy out in the open, and even had a few sips of wine after both my mother and Blanche assured her they'd drunk heavily throughout all their pregnancies, to no ill end.

Ron's color was high, and he seemed to truly enjoy all the stories of Uncle Wallace's millionaire clients–the Saudi prince who wanted a honeymoon in Vegas and rented the

Taj Mahal, the dot-com mogul who dreamed of riding camels through the desert. "I wanted to take Blanche to Italy for Christmas," said Uncle Wallace contemplatively.

"But look what I wanted instead," said Blanche, holding out her arm. On her wrist, a diamond bracelet flashed. I suddenly felt sorry for my mother, who had no one to give her jewels. I had given her a tin of Pat O'Brien's hurricane drink mix with two souvenir glasses.

We ate turkey and bread pudding and watched television in a sleepy stupor. When we were finally ready to drive back to Holt, my mother had drunk too many spritzers. She happened upon Remshart eating cookies in the kitchen and screamed, thinking he was a burglar. It was time to leave.

"I can see why you'd think that, Izzy," said Blanche as she led us out, "What with his hood over his head and that *do rag*."

The drive home was quiet. Both Madeline and my mother fell asleep, and Ron listened idly to soft rock. "I love Phil Collins," I said.

"Ugh," said Ron.

At home, after everyone had gone to bed, I sat next to the Christmas tree flipping through one of my mother's *W* magazines. I was supposed to fly back to New Orleans the next day. I had promised Jimbo that I would work New Year's, always a lucrative but bizarre night at The Highball.

I decided to go for a drive, pulling my mother's wool coat over my Christmas outfit and sliding my feet into Madeline's boots. We wore the same size in just about everything but pants, and now her pregnancy would equal out my late-night drinking and love of hot dogs. I stepped outside, and looked up at the dark sky.

In the garage, the Mercedes was still warm and smelled of my mother's perfume. I started the car, hoping I wouldn't wake anyone, and hit the button to open the garage door. I backed out of the driveway and drove by Mitchell, who was fast asleep again inside the guardhouse.

The streets of Holt were hushed, and I drove by homes with only Christmas lights burning, past Holt High School, the bank, and the library. I headed toward our old neighborhood, where we had lived when my father was alive, and Ellie was with us. I drove by our old house, large and quiet in the snowy night. How unhappy we had been in its high-ceilinged rooms.

I was wide awake on Christmas, and did not know where to go. There was a bar next to the train station, and I turned left, hoping it would be open. It was.

The Holt Grill had been fixed up: when I was younger, it had been called Holt Hamburgers. It had the best cheeseburgers in the world–thick, hand-formed patties–and the crispiest mozzarella sticks. I started hanging around bars when Ellie disappeared, and the smoky room in the back of Holt Hamburgers had been a place where I could always find someone to pour me a beer from their plastic pitcher.

Now, I had to walk through a room of tables with linen cloths to reach the bar, where there wasn't a pitcher in sight. I ordered a Scotch from the bartender, a teenager who looked Irish, and sat down on a stool. I couldn't see a jukebox, but Christmas carols played. There were a few small groups of dressed-up people. Did anyone in Holt ever wear sweatpants, I wondered. I always felt underdressed in my hometown, as well as underachieving. I sipped my drink, and then felt a hand on my shoulder.

"Hey," said Anthony, "I thought it was you."

Blood ran to my face; I could feel it. "Oh," I said, touching my cheek.

"I didn't mean to scare you," said Anthony, smiling. "Can I buy you a beer?"

"Scotch," I said, holding up my glass.

"Great," said Anthony. He looked over his shoulder to a group of people: his friends.

"Thanks for the champagne," I said.

"Oh," he shrugged. "New store policy."

"Really?" I stared into my drink.

"No," said Anthony. I looked back up, into his eyes. "My family's headed home," he said. His voice dropped. "They needed a little extra Christmas cheer," he whispered, rolling his eyes. I laughed. "Want to…go for a walk tomorrow?"

"Oh," I said, "OK." I thought, *a walk?*

"I'll come by. Around noon?"

"OK," I said. I smiled.

"Great," said Anthony.

I drove home slowly, through falling snowflakes. I thought about Anthony, and I felt a slow happiness, even after I had woken poor Mitchell and pulled into the warm garage.

My mother was in the living room, asleep on the couch next to the Christmas tree, snug in her quilted robe. On her lap was one of her folders, jammed with papers.

I took off my coat and smelled the smoke and beer from the bar in the folds of my clothes. I tried to take the boots off quietly. "Caroline?"

"Hey, Mom," I said, "I went for a walk."

"Come here, honey." My mother sat up straight, organizing her papers.

I walked toward her. "Mom, what are you doing in here? You should be in bed."

"Caroline, I need to talk to you," said my mother. She took her reading glasses from the side table and put them on.

"You sound serious," I said.

"I am serious. Sit down."

"Mom...."

"Keep your voice down," said my mother. I sat next to her, and she opened the folder. "I want you to listen until I'm finished," she said, "and don't tell me I'm crazy, OK?"

"OK, Mom, of course."

She took a deep breath. "Last year, I saw this picture in a magazine," she said. She lifted a brittle piece of paper, moved it under the light.

"Not another picture," I said, sighing.

"Caroline, this is different. Please, look." I looked. It was a picture of a Native American man in full garb, headdress and all. He was doing some sort of dance. The caption read: DANCING AT THE ARLEE RODEO.

"OK," I said.

"Do you see her?" said my mother.

"Her? It's a guy, a Native American, Mom. What's the deal?"

She pointed. "Look behind the Indian. Look at the crowd."

I scanned the crowd of people behind the man. They were blurry. I was trying to think of a nice way to tell my mother to let me go to bed when I saw her. Wearing jeans and a sleeveless shirt, the woman stood facing the camera. She wore her brown hair in a ponytail, and her face was lit up with laughter. I couldn't breathe. It was her grin. It was her.

"Where did you get this?"

"*People Magazine*," my mother said. "It's an article about Montana."

"It's her," I said.

I looked at my mother, and her face flooded with relief. "It is, isn't it?" she said. "My baby girl."

ELEVEN

from the desk of

AGNES FOWLER

Dear Louise,

Thank you for your Christmas card. And I hope you have a rockin' holiday season as well. I don't know how you know my father, but I suppose I should inform you that he is no longer with us. In other words, he is dead.

It happened about six months ago, Louise. It was a sunny afternoon, so I was walking home from school. I had just finished my Intro to James Joyce exam, and while I still didn't think I understood what the hey *Finnegans Wake* was all about, I had written an OK essay on *Portrait of the Artist as a Young Man*.

The point is, I was feeling relaxed.

My father and I lived together. I suppose I should have moved out, but I was the light of his life, as he always said.

I guess I liked being the light of someone's life.

On that June afternoon, I was thinking that maybe I would drag him out to dinner. He had become an inventor after the lumberyard closed, as I'm sure you know, and he spent entirely too much time alone in the basement. I was thinking the Bridge for pizza, or Piñata's in the mall.

I don't know why I remember, but I do: the sun had warmed the stones leading up to the front door. I took off my sandals and stood for a minute, feeling the heat on my toes and heels. I put my shoes back on to walk to the front door. My father did not approve of bare feet.

Well, there's no point in going into the depressing details. My father was in the basement. It looked as if he was asleep, his head down on his workbench. From the frame on his desk, my mother's picture gazed at him. A massive stroke, they told me.

So, this wasn't the most rockin' holiday season, if you really want to know. I was going to get a tree and a turkey, the same as every year, but I just didn't have it in me. I drank too much wine, watched hours of Christmas-themed television, and went to bed. One good thing about the television is that it doesn't take a vacation. It doesn't go to Disney World, like my supervisor Frances, or to Seattle to visit its brother, like Sally Beesley, the Reference Librarian. It stays right where you put it, ready to go.

Please don't send any flowers, Louise. I've finally gotten rid of all the flowers and the Tupperware containers.

Best to you,
Agnes Fowler

TWELVE

IT WAS THE DAY we were leaving for New Orleans. I sat smoking outside the senior hallway, watching the tennis team practice. The tennis team was symbolic of what I hated about Holt: all blond ponytails and earnestness. My mother was obsessed with tennis, and Madeline was on the middle school team. "My serve!" cried Kitty Jacobs, trotting prettily along in her shorts. I was terrible at tennis. I was a cheerleader, which consisted of smoking cigarettes and clapping. When my father deemed the $38 for my cheerleader skirt and sweater excessive, I could have used my own money, but I quit instead.

"I've got it!" cried the British exchange student, her skirt rising up as she reached for the ball.

I stood, ground out my cigarette with my toe, took a last look around, and left.

Stealing the Oldsmobile wasn't hard. When I got home, my mother was in bed, and the keys were in her purse. I stood in her bedroom doorway, watching her sleep. She was my mother, and

I loved her, but I loved my sisters more, and I had to choose.

I drove to school slowly, trying to burn my town into my memory. Madeline was waiting at the middle school. The other girls on the tennis team sat on the large rock outside the school giggling. Madeline stood a few feet from them, looking down, kicking at her racket. When I pulled in, she ran to the car. Nobody said goodbye to her; none of the tennis girls even turned. And wasn't she just as beautiful? Wasn't her ponytail perfect, and wasn't the way she tied her windbreaker around her waist just right? Madeline should have been the center of the circle of giggling girls, and I promised myself that in New Orleans she would be something wonderful.

"Damn," I said. "I forgot you had that racket."

"Maybe I'll play tennis in New Orleans," said Madeline.

"Maybe you will," I said.

Ellie was not waiting in front of Maxwell Elementary. She was supposed to meet us on the grassy strip in front of the parking lot. Usually, parents drove into the circular driveway, but we didn't want to risk being seen. I pulled to the curb and we waited.

"Where is she?" I said.

"I don't know," said Madeline. She was playing with her tennis racket, sticking her fingers through the holes. She took a breath and said, "I don't think we should run away."

"Shut up," I said.

Madeline began to whimper. She told me she and Ellie had had a fight. I told her to be quiet. She kicked the dashboard and turned her face away from me, her arms crossed over her chest.

After about a half an hour, every student was gone, and the parking lot was empty. Madeline and I stared at the vacant school. The jungle gym shone, and the swing set was still.

"What's going on?" said Madeline.

"I'm sure she got a ride," I said, though I wasn't sure of anything. "I'm sure she got a ride with Mrs. Lake," I said. I sighed, and started the car.

"What are we going to do?" said Madeline.

"I guess we're going home."

I looked for Ellie as I drove. Maybe, I thought, she had missed me, maybe waited in another spot and then walked home. I was annoyed, but not upset, really. All my adrenaline—all the energy that had gone into planning our escape—was deflated, and I felt flat as a pancake, tired.

I squinted against the late-afternoon sun, and searched for my sister along the dappled sidewalks of Maxwell Avenue. I slowed and peered into the windows of the Seafood Shack, where we went once in a while for fried shrimp.

Down Sycamore Lane and through Hillside Village, we looked for her. Madeline was silent in the passenger seat. She rolled the window down partway, her fingers curled around the top, and she focused intently, trying to find Ellie. There was a terrible feeling in my stomach. I began to feel as if things had gone very wrong. I just wanted to see Ellie, her toothless smile. I was supposed to be her hero: we should have been flying down I-95 toward bliss.

I parked the Oldsmobile and walked into the house, Madeline trailing behind me. Our mother was sitting in the kitchen and scribbling into her journal.

"Where have you been?" she said, fixing us with a bleary stare.

"Madeline's tennis," I said.

"Oh, no!" said my mother. "Did I miss a tournament?"

"No," said Madeline flatly.

"Did I hear the garage door?" said my mother, glancing at me. I shook my head. "Mrs. Lake just dropped us off," I said.

"Where's Ellie?" said Madeline.

My mother pursed her lips. I could see her trying to think. "What do you mean?" she said.

"Where's Ellie?" I said. "We mean, where's Ellie?"

"I thought she was with you girls," said my mother. "I figured...."

She didn't finish her sentence. We stood in the kitchen, immobile. The day's light was fading, and long shadows came in from the windows and sliding glass door. My mother closed her notebook. "Maybe she's asleep," she said, doubtfully.

We began to call her name. We hunted through the house, in every room. We piled back in the Oldsmobile and drove around the neighborhood, calling for her, as if she were a lost puppy. When we got home, my mother called the police, and I took our pillowcases out of the car and unpacked them, putting the outfit I had imagined I would wear to my New Orleans job back on a hanger, stashing Ellie's Gummi bears in her sock drawer.

That night, I woke, and Madeline was standing in my doorway. "I'm scared," she said, "Can I sleep with you?" I peeled back the covers, and Madeline climbed in. I thought about Ellie, who slept on her side, her knees drawn to her chest, the blanket pulled close to her face. Madeline and I huddled next to each other, trying to get warm.

We waited at home. I guess I expected a message from Ellie, a secret sign. Maybe I had screwed up the plan, I thought: had I told her to meet us somewhere else? I had a dream that she was waiting behind the dogwood tree in our yard, but no one was there when I checked in the morning. I sat in my closet with my eyes closed and my fingertips to my temples, thinking so hard I got dizzy. What had I missed? Where had I gone wrong? It was always clear to me that her disappearance was my fault.

The next morning, we took the police to Maxwell Elementary, watched while they interviewed teachers and kids who might have seen her. Police combed our town. People would answer their doors smiling, and then their hands would go to their mouths or to the wall for support as they heard about Ellie. We stayed home from school and our father stayed home from work, sitting in the den and drinking. My mother snapped out of her lethargy and began a frenzied search that would possess her for the rest of her life. She made photocopies of a picture of Ellie at Pronto Printer in Port Chester and tacked them up all over town. She called every person in the Holt phone book from a neighbor's house, starting with the "A's" and moving through the alphabet.

After two days, the policeman assigned to Ellie's case seemed nervous. He was a young blond man, with pale skin and blue eyes. When he talked to my mother and she began to cry, it looked like he would cry, too.

We found out later that after forty-eight hours, the chances of finding someone drop significantly. Ellie's picture was on the news and in the paper. Reporters surrounded our house. I could hear them late at night, opening beers and laughing on our lawn. In the morning, they drank coffee from paper cups.

THIRTEEN

BY THE LIGHT of the Christmas tree, my mother's face glowed. "Can you find her?" she asked me. "Maybe you could go out there to…," she looked down at the clipping, "Arlee, Montana. I'll pay anything."

"Mom, it can't really be her," I said, though my heart was hammering in my chest.

"But what if it is?"

I shook my head, and stared at the picture. The girl looked like me, like Madeline. She looked like my mother, those crinkles around her eyes. And her hair was the same color Ellie's had been: light brown, with slices of gold. "This was last year?" I said.

My mother nodded. "Think about it," she said. "I know it seems crazy. But before we…before we let that lawyer… shouldn't we be sure?"

"I can't just leave," I said, lamely.

"I know, honey," said my mother. "It would be for me," she added.

*

After she went to bed, I stared at the picture for a while. In some ways, I felt like Madeline did: if Ellie were alive, laughing at some fucking rodeo, why wouldn't she have called us?

I was exhausted. I did not want to think about Ellie. I went upstairs and changed into my nightgown. I lay in bed for some time before I finally fell asleep.

Her breath whispered across my face: *Caroline.* I felt her kiss on my forehead. *Goodbye, Caroline.* I struggled toward consciousness, swimming upward, opening my eyes.

"Ellie?" I said.

Madeline looked startled. "No, it's me," she said. She brushed my hair back from my forehead with her fingers. "Just me," she said. I blinked.

"Am I awake?" I said.

"Don't know," said Madeline, "but Ron and I are off. Have a safe trip back, Care."

I sat up, but did not reach for my sister. There was so much we hadn't talked about, so much unsaid, but I didn't stop her as she pressed her lips to my cheek and walked away, leaving a lipstick goodbye.

When I came downstairs showered and wearing mascara my mother almost dropped the paper. "Sweetie!" she said, "Look at you!"

"Hi, Mom."

"Well! I was thinking we could hit the day-after-Christmas sales. We can start at the Galleria, and then work our way to Bloomingdale's and Neiman's. We can even have lunch...," her voice trailed off. "Caroline?"

I looked up. "What?" I said.

"You look like you're a million miles away."

"Oh," I blushed, "it's just that...well, I sort of have...an appointment."

My mother narrowed her eyes. "A hair appointment?"

"No...."

She raised an eyebrow. "A manicure?" I shook my head. Her face burst open like a flower. "A *date*?" she screeched.

"Mom, it's not really a date."

"Hold on!" my mother was practically shaking. She ran to the toaster. "Let me make some English muffins. I want *all the details*!" She expertly pulled two muffins apart and jammed them in. "Butter? Honey?" she said.

"Sure, Mom, but there aren't really any...."

She held up her hand like a traffic cop. "Wait!" she cried. "Let's wait until we have muffins and fresh cups of coffee."

I began to laugh. After my father's death, my mother had grown younger, it seemed, becoming more and more like the woman he had met on a blind date, full of the spirit and energy he and Ellie's disappearance had drained out of her. She waited impatiently for the muffins to toast, and then put them on china plates, spreading thick layers of butter and honey. She refilled her coffee cup and then mine, sitting at the kitchen table and patting the chair next to her. "I'm ready!" she said. I had never told her about a date before. I had never told her much of anything. I smiled.

"It all began at the Christmas party," I said.

*

By the time Anthony arrived, my mother had convinced me to apply Plum Passion eye shadow and Peachy Keen lipstick. She had done my nails, slid gold studs into my earlobes. Off came my T-shirt and jeans, replaced with a pastel sweater set and corduroy pants. No to the Converse high tops, yes to tasseled loafers. I heard my mother chattering as I descended the stairs. Anthony was sitting on the pink loveseat, a mug of cider in his hand and a plate of ginger cookies on his lap. "Here she is now," said my mother, standing up, appraising me from top to bottom, and nodding approvingly.

Anthony was wearing jeans and hiking boots.

"Hi," I said.

"Hey," said Anthony. He was looking straight into my eyes, and he couldn't seem to keep from smiling. He stood, the plate of cookies falling from his lap and shattering on the floor. "Oh, God," he said.

"No, no. No problem. Don't worry!" chirped my mother, running for the broom.

"I'm so sorry," he said.

"It's OK, really," I said.

"Um, you look great," said Anthony.

"Really?"

"Yeah. But you might want some galoshes."

"Galoshes?" I smiled.

"I mean, boots. I don't know. I thought we could take a walk. In the snow."

"Would sneakers be OK?"

"Sure. I just don't want you to ruin, um, your...penny loafers."

I ran into the kitchen to kiss my mom goodbye. "Why are you wearing those hideous *shoes*?" she whispered fervently.

"I'll explain later," I told her.

Anthony drove a truck. I climbed in, nearly splitting the seams of my mother's expensive pants. "Are we going somewhere I can wear cashmere?" I asked. Anthony looked nervous. "Hey," I said, "I'm kidding. My mother dressed me."

He raised his eyebrows and breathed out hard. He shook his head. "Holt girls," he said.

"Winters girls," I said. "Did you know Madeline in high school?"

Anthony waved to Mitchell and drove past the guardhouse, turning left. "She was a few years younger," said Anthony, "but I knew who she was."

"Because of Ellie," I said.

"Well," said Anthony.

"And my dad," I said.

"It's a small town," said Anthony. He put his hand on my knee, and I did not move it. "I heard about you, too," he said, "the wild Caroline Winters."

"What?"

"You left quite an impression when you went away to boarding school," said Anthony.

"Come on."

He looked at me. "Caroline," he said, "are you kidding?"

"Jesus." I had hardly thought about what had gone on

back in Holt after I left.

"Anyway," said Anthony, "don't you want to know the plan?"

"I fly back to New Orleans tonight," I said, "so I can't be gone too long."

Anthony nodded. "I'm sorry if I upset you," he said, gently.

"No, I'm fine."

Anthony didn't say anything for a while. He drove to the Holt Nature Center and parked the car. "Here we are," he said. He opened the door and took my hand. As I climbed from the car, he pulled me toward him, folding me in his arms. "I'm sorry," he said. His arms felt good, but I was stiff. I wanted to be back in New Orleans, talking to Georgette in my apartment on Esplanade. I did not want to be at the Nature Center with some liquor store owner. The more I thought about it, the more I realized how much Anthony must have known about my family: my father bought the bottles that killed him at the Liquor Barn. Anthony went to high school with Madeline, and had probably spent more time with my mother in the past years than I had.

Anthony let me go. He reached into the bed of the truck and brought out a picnic basket. It was the old-fashioned kind, woven and latched on top. "Come on," said Anthony, "I won't talk any more."

He walked in front of me, and I followed. Our steps made crunching sounds in the snow. I saw footprints–rabbits? deer?–but since the last snowfall, we were the only people to walk the trail. I hadn't spent much time at the Nature Center, save an occasional elementary school trip. Moving my legs felt wonderful, my sluggish blood finally circulating.

After walking for a while, we reached a clearing. “How are you doing in those wet sneakers?” he said.

“Fine.”

He stopped next to a bench in a sunny spot. “Is it too cold for you?” he said.

“No.”

He sat down and opened the basket. “I hope you're hungry,” he said. I nodded, sitting next to him.

He pulled a crusty loaf of bread from the basket. “Good, still hot,” he said, and handed it to me. “I've been cooking all morning,” he said shyly.

“You cook?”

“I do.”

Another container held grapes, and one a lasagna. Finally, Anthony took a large, unlabeled bottle from the basket. “I have some great wines,” he said, “but I knew you liked beer. This is the Anthony Sorrento special.”

“Sorry?”

“I brewed it myself. Last fall. It's a stout. I hope you're not a beer connoisseur.”

“No,” I said, “I'm used to cans, actually. Budweiser.”

He opened the bottle and poured me a glass. It tasted thick and heavy. “I love it,” I said.

“I'm so glad. I've got lots.” He unlatched a strap that held plates, spread a napkin on my lap, and handed me a serving spoon. “Have at it,” he said.

We ate in a comfortable silence. It was a warm December day, and I could hear an occasional car from the road. The food was delicious: oregano, tomato, hot bread with butter, tart grapes, and the heavy beer. "So what's your story?" I said, finally.

Anthony lay back on the blanket, propped his head up with one elbow. "I grew up here, as you know. Played football for the Holt Hammerheads. Scholarship to Cornell, and then I stayed at Cornell for graduate school. I had grand plans of opening a restaurant on some tropical island, but my dad asked me to come back and take over the store. I guess I thought I'd do it for a few years and then go…see the world, like you have. I'm the oldest of six, thought one of my brothers would take it over." He sighed. "It didn't work out that way."

"I can't believe you're not married," I said. He was silent. I added, "I mean, everyone in Holt seems to be."

"I was," said Anthony. His face darkened.

"Oh," I said, "I'm sorry. I didn't …"

"She was a manager at Windows on the World," said Anthony, his voice catching. "Jennifer. I met her at Cornell. The plan was to save for a few years, then open our own place somewhere…amazing. At night, we'd look at maps, trying to pick the spot. It was going to be called Sorrento's by the Sea."

"I'm so sorry," I said, "I didn't know."

"She was at work on the eleventh, as usual. When the first plane hit, she called the store, but I was in the back. My brother Danny took the message. She said she loved me. By the time I called back, it was…there was no answer."

"Jesus," I said. I reached toward Anthony, but did not

know where to touch him, and I let my hand drop. He was looking at his napkin, tracing one of the plaid squares. I sipped my beer.

"Some date, huh?" he said, sitting up and wiping his eyes.

"It's a perfect date," I said. He leaned toward me, and I kissed him. His lips were soft, and his mouth tasted of beer. He took my face in his hands as we kissed, then ran his fingers down my neck to my breast. He unbuttoned my mother's coat slowly, kissing my eyelids, my cheeks, my lips. He moved his warm hand underneath the ridiculous sweater set. A thick shock ran through me, and I felt small and light in his arms. He wrapped himself around me, his mouth on mine, and until he stopped, pulled back, it was as if we were one person, tangled in wool and hot breath.

FOURTEEN

"What the fuck?" I said to Madeline, when my mother told us she was heading to bed at four in the afternoon. Madeline shrugged. We were watching television in the kitchen. It had been a year since Ellie's disappearance, and my mother had worn a bathrobe for most of it.

My new motto was "What the fuck." I wrote it on all my notebooks, which were in my school locker. I had not been to school in weeks. By taking whatever drugs they gave me and paying for them, I had gathered a group of friends around me. We went to each others' houses and ate mushrooms in our parents' wood-paneled basements. We snorted lines of Ritalin, cutting it with our fathers' razorblades on our mothers' decorating magazines.

That night, I went out on Hugh King's boat. I liked the way the boat slapped against the water as Hugh drove it too fast. I liked the warmth of Hugh's father's Glenfiddich in my mouth. Hugh dropped me off late, and I walked around to the side of the house, planning to slip in the sliding glass door. Usually, my parents were both dead to the world by then, but that night, they were awake. I was walking past the den window when I heard them talking. I slid down to the grass, crossed my legs, and listened.

"I have one question for you, Isabelle." My father's voice was slow and slurred.

"What?" said my mother. She sounded empty.

"Was she even mine?"

My mother said, "Of course! Joseph, my God!"

Again, there was a silence. Suddenly full of energy, I stood and ran across the lawn. I cartwheeled, and landed with my cheek to the grass, breathing hard. There were no stars in the sky. I said, I don't care. I don't care. I don't care.

The next night, I went to a party in a hotel room in White Plains. There was a game, and when you lost, you drank a shot of vodka. Vodka didn't taste like anything. The nothing taste slipped down my throat. I went into the bathroom, a hotel bathroom with a thick bathmat to rest my head on. I woke up in the hospital.

My ribs hurt; the paramedics pounded hard enough to start my heart. Soon afterward, I was sent to boarding school, where I learned to dip tobacco and give blow jobs.

FIFTEEN

from the desk of

AGNES FOWLER

Dear Louise,

Thank you for clarifying your relationship to my departed father. He certainly did love shopping at Rockin' Rudy's Record Store. I plan to keep his collection as it is for now. I like to listen to his records and think of the way he'd sing along. I sang along, too, and sometimes he'd stop singing and just look at me. Did I mention how much he loved me?

I will contact you if I do decide to sell. But I doubt it.

All best,
Agnes Fowler

P.S. Thanks a lot for the flowers.

SIXTEEN

"WELL, SOMEBODY GOT SOME BOOTY," said Winnie, when I walked into The Highball on Wednesday.

"What?" I said, sipping my takeout coffee from CC's.

"I can tell a million miles away, sister," said Winnie, "and as soon as I serve this mo-fo, I want to know every dirty detail." I shook my head, laughing, and went into Jimbo's office.

"I'm back," I said. Jimbo was drinking from a Christmas mug.

"Good thing," he said. "How was the Big Apple?"

"I'm from the suburbs, actually," I said.

"Hmph," said Jimbo. He wore a three-piece suit, as usual. "Now listen, Caroline," he said, "are you listening?"

I nodded.

"I've got a potential buyer coming in for New Year's," Jimbo said. "Some fashion model and her husband. They want to redo the place, make it a movie star hangout."

I looked toward the group coming in the door, about twenty people wearing sun visors and T-shirts that said

WEIGHT WATCHERS NEW ORLEANS. "It's pretty glamorous already," I said.

"Ha ha," said Jimbo dryly. "Now, Caroline, are you listening?"

"Yes, Jimbo."

"New Year's Eve, I want you glamorized to the max," said Jimbo. "Is that clear?"

"Glamorized to the max."

He leaned back, pleased. "I'm ready to retire," he said. "Spent my whole life in this shithole of a city, in this shithole of a bar. A revolving shithole. I'm getting out. I'm going to buy a condo in Celebration, Florida. Did you know that, Caroline?"

"Yes, Jimbo. You told me."

"Designed by Disney. The whole city planned out. Organized. Clean." He leaned back in his chair. "No tourists," he added happily, and then he poured more whiskey into his Christmas mug.

Winnie offered to buy Peggy and me drinks if I would share the dirt. I agreed. After work, we headed to Bobby's Bar in Winnie's Cadillac. Peggy had never been to Bobby's before. "I told Len I needed a night out with the girls," she said. "Fancy drinks. Nice clothes. Like *Sex and the City*. I'm Samantha." Peggy was so skinny we all wondered if she ate, but her shoulders were huge from doing headstands at yoga class. She wore leotards and tights much of the time, as if on the way to aerobics class, and not a bar.

"I don't think they have fancy drinks at Bobby's," I said.

Winnie raised an eyebrow. “They’ve got Courvoisier,” she said. “Damn!” Winnie wore her winter coat, which was aqua-colored. On her finger, a new ring from Kit flashed. Kit screwed up often, forgetting to come home, dancing with the wrong woman, buying beer with the rent money. To gain Winnie’s forgiveness, he bought her lots of jewelry, and Winnie liked to wear all her jewelry at once. Winnie had four children, one of whom was Kit’s. Kit had two children of his own. They all lived in a big ramshackle house over the border in Mississippi.

We drove out of the business district toward my house. “Have you ever heard of the Red Lounge?” said Peggy. “Maybe we should go there. They have roses on all the tables.”

Bobby’s Bar was on the outskirts of Tremé, next to an underpass. Winnie parked the Cadillac and affixed The Club to the steering wheel. “Where *are* we?” said Peggy. Nobody answered.

From the outside, Bobby’s looks like nothing much. There are a few neon beer signs in the window, and the BOBBY’S BAR sign is falling down. On the inside, it looks like nothing much filled with very drunk people and a great jukebox. “I get it,” said Peggy. “We’re in the black part of town. I’m with you. It’s cool. Are we going to hear some jazz?”

Winnie was a regular at Bobby’s. Kit was already at a table with three men and four bottles of Seagram’s VO. He stood up when we walked in, and Winnie touched the collar of her yellow blouse. “Ladies!” called Kit.

“Oh God,” said Peggy, taking in the broken tables, the remains of the Wednesday Catfish Fry on the bartop.

Winnie sashayed over to Kit, planting a big one on his mouth. "I'm with the girls tonight," she said.

"Winnie the Pooh!" said Kit.

"Caroline got some nookie," whispered Winnie, though I could hear, as could the rest of the bar. "And I gotta get the details. I'll tell you later."

"Nookie, huh?" said Kit.

"Winnie, Jesus!" I said. I sat down at an empty table, and Peggy sat next to me. Winnie, after making out with Kit for a while, bought six tall boys and joined us. Peggy cracked her can open with resignation.

"This is *nothing* like *Sex and the City*," she said. "This is like staying home drinking beer with Len." Peggy's boyfriend, Len, was a self-proclaimed artist. He had not yet figured out his medium, however, and spent his time getting stoned on their front porch and strumming a broken guitar. Peggy fed stray dogs and cats, and the Bywater house she shared with Len was full of fleas.

"Do you have a jukebox at home?" asked Winnie. She was getting angry, I could tell.

"No," said Peggy.

"Here," said Winnie, handing Peggy some change. "Go on," she said. Peggy walked with trepidation to the jukebox, where she was quickly approached by a thin boy wearing a telephone headset that was not attached to anything.

"How could you tell?" I whispered.

Winnie threw her head back and laughed. "Honey," she said, "you are oozing sex-u-ality like a sponge."

"Yuck," I said.

"Spill it," said Winnie.

"His name is Anthony," I said. "He owns a liquor store."

"Score!" said Winnie. "I like him already."

I blushed. "He's tall. He has blue eyes. His wife was killed on September 11."

"Jay-sus!"

I nodded. "He's…I don't know."

"Sex?" said Winnie.

"Sorry?"

"Sex!" said Winnie, loudly.

From his table, Kit said, "Winnie the *Pooh*!"

I put my hands to my face. "No," I said, "not yet."

"Did you make out with him, at least?"

I peeked from between my fingers. "Yes."

"Score!" said Winnie. "Tongue?" I nodded. "Tongue!" cried Winnie happily. Men began to gather around our table. Music spilled from the jukebox: the Mardi Gras Indians. The Mardi Gras Indians were men and boys who dressed up for the parades and played music. The tradition of the Indians had begun as a way to get in on the snooty Mardi Gras festivities. Each year, they made elaborate beaded costumes, sewing by hand on bartops and kitchen tables. Peggy rushed back to us.

"I figured I'd play the Indians," she said. "You know, it sort of fits in." She began to move her shoulders to the chanting beat. Suddenly, the music stopped. Someone had pulled the plug from the jukebox. It was a large black woman, who plugged the box back in and then filled it with quarters, lining up ten Barry White songs in a row.

"Did somebody say tongue?" said Kit, coming up behind Winnie and leaning in toward her.

The phone woke me the next morning. My head felt like cement. Next to me, Georgette stretched out, yawning. My next-door neighbors had taken good care of her while I was gone for Christmas—she looked to have gained ten pounds. How had I gotten home?

I reached for the receiver. "Hello? Hello?"

"Caroline? It's Anthony." My breath caught. "Um, from the Liquor Barn?" he said.

"I know," I said. "Sorry, I had a late night. I'm a little discombobulated."

"Discombobulated, huh?"

"Yeah."

"What did you do?" he asked.

"Oh, just went out with some girlfriends."

"Well, I just wanted to, um, make sure you got home safely."

"I did. Thanks," I said.

"And how is everything at The Cue Ball?"

"The Highball?"

"Yeah, sorry."

"Hey, Anthony?"

"Yes?"

"Could I call you back when I've had some coffee?"

He laughed, a rich sound. "Actually, why don't you think about something while you have your coffee," he said.

"Shoot."

He drew a breath. "I miss you," he said. "So I bought a ticket to New Orleans. For New Year's."

I felt a burning in my stomach. "What?"

"I'm booked in a hotel downtown," said Anthony. "Don't worry. In fact, if you don't want to see me, that's fine. Well, it's not fine, but I...." There was a pause. "I've decided recently to become an impulsive person," he said, "and I've always wanted to see New Orleans."

"I'll, uh, let me call you back," I said.

"Oh," said Anthony. I could tell he was disappointed. "OK. I'll, well, I'll be waiting here by the phone."

I laughed, but it sounded fake. "Bye," I said, and hung up. Outside my apartment, I heard a wail of horns, and then a crash. "Fuck," I said. I opened my front door, grabbed the *Times-Picayune,* and slammed the door without seeing the accident. I went into the kitchen and poured water in the coffeemaker, added six spoonfuls of coffee. I put food in Georgette's bowl, and then opened the paper.

I couldn't concentrate, and my stomach was queasy. The phone rang again. *Jesus,* I thought. I picked it up. "Hello?"

"Care?" It was Madeline.

"Hey," I said. "What's going on?"

"Oh, I don't know."

The coffee was ready, and I poured a black cup and sipped it. "Are you OK?" I asked.

"Not really. No, I'm fine. You know. I guess it's the hormones or something."

"Hm," I said. Madeline never called me to chat. I waited for the reason.

"Look," said Madeline, "I met with Ken Dowland yesterday. I know you don't want to deal with this. But Ken's going to trial in March and Mom won't help him."

"Oh," I said. I made a face at Georgette. This was too much in the morning! I looked at the clock. It was two p.m.

"Care, I know she showed you the picture. I've seen it, too."

"Uh-huh."

"Caroline, come on. How could Ellie have possibly…I mean, Montana?"

"I don't know, Maddy."

"Well, none of us do," Madeline's voice flared in anger. "Then go find her! I don't care, but this has got to end someday. Jesus."

I stared at my fingernails. Finally, Madeline spoke evenly. "Look. My therapist says I need closure. I do. She's dead, and we all know it. I can go to the courts without Mom, and I will. I wanted you all to be involved. I thought…."

"What?" I said. "You thought *what*?"

"Did it ever occur to you that your whole life is on hold?" said Madeline. "Have you ever taken a look at yourself? You're just…treading water, waiting for Ellie to come back."

"That's not true."

"Think about it," said Madeline. "I'm sorry to be harsh. You need to do what you need to do, and if you want to wait forever, I guess that's not my business. But I have to do this, so I can move on."

"What? You don't think I want to move on?" I said shrilly.

"Caroline, there are people right here who need you. And she's never coming back."

My eyes filled with tears. "I don't know," I said.

After a cheeseburger at the Camellia Grill, I walked to the levee, hiking along a trail to the water and sitting down on a tree stump. People walked their dogs along the riverbank, but it was blissfully empty midday. The sun beat down on me, and I watched a barge on the Mississippi. I was next to some sort of junkyard, filled with broken metal parts, but if I looked straight ahead I saw only the water rolling past. I could pretend it wasn't polluted, filled with oil.

Of course I knew what might have happened to my baby sister. I didn't like to think about the worst possibilities: a strong hand yanking at her hair, a palm against her throat. A hard body against her soft one, invading her, a knife, her blood spilling. Everything burned but her bones. I saw visions of her open mouth, fear inside her eyes.

When my father turned James O'Hara away at the door, I ran upstairs and wept. I cried, convulsing sobs, knowing I would never be normal, and my father's grip would never fade. Ellie came upstairs and heard me. She lay next to me and pressed her body along mine, her arms around my waist.

If she had lived, she would have called me. For sixteen years, I had waited. Sometimes, I knew she was dead with a certainty that felt like truth. But sometimes, I stood at the window, willing her to turn the corner, to knock on my door.

My mother phoned when I got home. She told me all about the Randalls' party, the roast beef, the baked brie. "I had a bit too much vino," she said, "but what the hey, it's Christmas."

"Well, not anymore, technically," I said.

"Don't be a sourpuss," she said.

"Who, um...."

"Yes?"

"Who was the bartender? Was he from the Liquor Barn?" I asked.

"No, it was some Randall cousin. But I'm going over there today. Can I give a message to Anthony?"

"No."

"Are you sure?"

"Mom!" Her coy tone infuriated me. "Actually," I said, "there is something I'd like you to tell him. Would you tell him I have a boyfriend?"

"You do?" said my mother.

"No," I admitted, "but I don't want Anthony to get the wrong idea, you know?"

"The wrong idea? Are you crazy? He's a fine boy, Anthony. Honestly, Caroline, what's the matter with you?" I was silent. "OK, whatever you say," said my mother. "I'll tell him to give up on you."

"Thanks."

"Honestly!" said my mother.

"Well, have a good New Year's," I said. She jabbered on about the new outfit she had bought at Saks to wear to the party at the golf club–a dress with feathers–and then she got off the phone, telling me to buck up.

SEVENTEEN

from the desk of

AGNES FOWLER

Dear Johan,

I should probably begin by saying that I have never done this before. I mean, I have written letters before—many of them—but not to a man. Well, that's not truly accurate. I had a pen pal in the Ukraine whose name was Vladimir. My father read in *Home School Your Precious Child* that pen pals were advantageous to home-schooled kids, so he contacted Positively Pen Pals from their advertisement in the back of *Highlights*. They hooked me up with a student at Kharkiv High School. Unfortunately, Vladimir could not read English very well (they have a different alphabet, which was news to me!) and so I only got a few, dull letters back, most of them reporting on the status of Vladimir's many pets. I kept writing anyway. Well, and the point is, I hope I get a letter back from you. And Vladimir wasn't a man, anyway, just a boy.

I found your name (and saw your picture) on AlaskaHunks.com. I hope you don't think I go around surfing the web for available men. I'm not really very talented at finding things on the web the way Sally Beesley, the Reference Librarian, is. You can ask Sally any question and she will find you the answer on the web. Just yesterday, Frances (my supervisor) asked Sally what on earth she could cook with zucchini and Sally printed out three recipes lickety-split and one of them was even a dessert! (Chocolate Zucchini Cake.)

I found out about AlaskaHunks.com from Frances, actually, the one with the zucchini. She came in Monday morning and walked right over to my cubby and said, "Agnes, we're going to find you a boyfriend and we're going to do it right now." I didn't know what to say. It is certainly not that I am desperate. In fact I very much like my life the way it is. I have a cozy home on Daly Avenue. I can eat pancakes for dinner if I want, and I can eat pizza for breakfast. But I digress.

Frances (the one with the zucchini) saw the *Sixty Minutes* all about AlaskaHunks.com. She told me there were many smart, handsome men in Alaska and not very many women. She told me about the Love Match Vacation Packages, and the three women from Wisconsin who had married "hot honeys." (These were Frances' words, Johan—I don't say things like "hot honeys," and certainly not in the officeplace.)

"You like the cold, and you can be a librarian anywhere," said Frances. "Log on and let's go," she said. I felt a bit uncomfortable, especially as many of the other librarians had surrounded my cubby. "Shove over, Grover," said Frances, and she pulled up a chair, pushed my stack of OCLC search cards aside, and logged on to the web. She typed in: AlaskaHunks.com, and she began to read.

Of course I told them I was absolutely NOT interested! Honestly. I have plenty of dates here in Missoula. Just last week, I had coffee with Bruce Upchurch. He was installing my laminated flooring at the time, but we had coffee, and Entenmann's Raspberry Twist coffee cake.

It was later, when everyone went into the Break Room to celebrate Jon Davies' birthday, that I took a peek at the AlaskaHunks.com web site. I could hear them all singing "How old are you now..." which is entirely inappropriate, as Jon Davies is not a spring chicken. The poor man has been in charge of the Montana History Room for as long as anyone can remember. He sits amongst his dusty basement shelves, and nobody ever comes down to say hey-ho. Most students just don't care about Montana history. They are all about the present, ordering articles about the Human Genome Project and Leonardo DiCaprio. But again, I digress.

There was a place on the web page to put your name and address, so I did. Nothing wrong with getting a catalog in the mail, is what I thought, even if it was a catalog of MEN. (I don't know why I capitalized that–MEN. I have had two and a half glasses of Chardonnay, so perhaps I should take a break. Or have some milk.)

Things went on as usual.

On Friday, I came home after work to find a crisp brown envelope in my mailbox. (I have a snazzy mailbox, Johan. It's a regular, metal box, but then I've added a fish tail and a fish head, made out of wood. I conceived of the whole project one night after four glasses of Chardonnay. *Quel succès!* I speak French.)

The catalog from AlaskaHunks.com is pretty thick. This is not to say that you are not a friendly looking and I must even say handsome man. But jeez, there are many hunks in Alaska, was what I thought as I flipped through the catalog. I looked briefly at the Love Match Vacation Package section, and though the cruise ship looks very glamorous and the 24-hour buffet especially appealing, I don't think I could take ten days off from work and I like to write letters anyway.

Be right back–must go to Orange Street Food Farm for more Chardonnay and coffee cake.

It's a beautiful night here in Missoula. Whispery and cold and white. Sometimes winter can be depressing, what with the smell from the paper mill, but tonight is beautiful. I left footprints in the snow as I walked to the Orange Street Food Farm, and I followed them home. Where was I?

So, my Love Jumpstart Activation Fee entitled me to two Alaskan hunks' addresses. I want you to know that I only asked for one.

I suppose I should tell you a bit about myself. I work in InterLibrary Loan at the University of Montana Mansfield

Library. (I don't know why they capitalize that "L" in "InterLibrary Loan." It looks wrong to me, but I don't make the rules.) My job entails searching for books and articles that library patrons have requested. Some days, this is dull. Other days, it's fascinating, such as when I found a rare book about spinal meningitis at a library in Perth, Australia, and got to call them and hear their accents. I have not traveled far and wide, though I have been to Spokane and also to Coeur D'Alene, Idaho, on the Dinner Theater Bus. (The show was *Cats.* Have you seen it? The songs are morose but the cat dancing is really inspired. I bought the tape and would be happy to lend it to you, or maybe you can just buy it there. I assume they have music stores in Skagway! I also got a T-shirt signed by three of the cat actors.)

My favorite food is pancakes. I love candy, especially Gummi bears. I prefer Chardonnay and martinis on special occasions, though olives are not my favorite. I read an article in *Bon Appétit* about a bar in New York City where you can get a martini with a little hot pepper in it, instead of an olive or one of those pickled onions. How about a huckleberry? That's what I'd like to know.

My favorite place is in front of my fireplace reading a magazine. In the summer, my favorite place is in my hammock reading a magazine.

My pen is running out of ink! I hope you can read my handwriting–I know it slants a bit to the side, hope you're not a handwriting analyst. Who knows what the loops in my W's say.

I'm feeling shy now, as I come to the end of this letter.

I'm not really even sure what I want to happen—or if I want you to write me back. Of course I want you to write me back, but I also like my life the way it is. I'm not sure why I'm doing this, is what I'm saying. Like I said, I've never done anything like this before.

You might want to know why I chose you out of all the other hunks. Well, write back and I will tell you.

Yours sincerely,
Agnes Fowler

EIGHTEEN

THE DOORBELL in my New Orleans apartment was loud. I pulled a T-shirt over my nightgown, and ran down the stairs. I threw the door open, and on my porch, holding a garment bag over his shoulder, was Anthony. "What?" I said.

"Your mother told me to come right away," he said, "and she sent this dress. It has feathers." He handed me the bag. I touched my hair. "Can I come in?" he asked.

"Sure," I said. "Did she really tell you to come?"

"Well, she said you didn't have a dress for New Year's, or a date."

"Christ!"

I was flustered and embarrassed. I gave Anthony the paper to read while I showered, and then sat down at the kitchen table in a sundress, my feet bare, my hair wet. Anthony was still in his coat. It was way too heavy for New Orleans. I could hear the pipes through the walls, and some Hindu music from next door. "You never called me back," said Anthony.

"Yeah," I said.

"You don't want me here, do you?" he said. He sounded as if he was getting angry. I picked up my cup, and then put it down. I lifted my shoulders and tried to speak, but nothing came out. I remembered his lips, his warm hands on my skin. I wanted to reach for him, but something stopped me.

"It's OK," said Anthony. "I made a mistake. I thought there was something...but I guess there isn't."

"I'm sorry," I said. "I don't...."

"Never mind," said Anthony. He stood up. "Fuck," he said. He went to the door, and let himself out. I listened to his footsteps as he walked down the staircase. I did not go to the window to watch him walk away. Now I was alone, which is what I had wanted. But I didn't feel better: I missed him.

"Do you mean to tell me you could have spent the whole day in bed with an Italian?" said Winnie, applying glitter to her eyelids. I shrugged, and the feathers at my neckline tickled my chin. "You need some sweet loving, girl," said Winnie, "or some therapy."

"Did you ever feel like Kit was too good for you? Too much...I don't know. Like he wanted something from you that you didn't know if you could give?"

Winnie snorted. "Kit? Too good for *me*? Are you drunk?"

I was, a bit, but I said, "Forget it."

"And what's *up* with that dress? You some sort of bird, Caroline?"

"It's from Saks Fifth Avenue," I said.

"You gonna fly off the top of this building?" said Winnie,

cracking up at her joke.

Peggy burst into the bathroom. In her gold lamé dress, she looked fabulous. "Check it out," she said, lifting the hem to reveal gold, thigh-high boots. "They were having a sale at Naughty Nancy's." She looked up, and her brow furrowed. "Are you wearing that?" she said.

"It's from Saks Fifth Avenue," I said.

"Yikes," said Peggy.

Winnie said, "Did it fly here itself?" and they both laughed uproariously.

Jimbo gathered us in front of the bar. "Here's the deal, my glamour girls," he said, rubbing his hands together. "Crystal Robbins and her boyfriend will be here at eleven. The boyfriend is the developer. He's already opened bars in New York, Miami, and L.A. He's looking to make The Highball a hotspot."

I looked at Jimbo's decorations: giant cardboard martinis hanging from the ceiling, fake presents under a scraggly tree, centerpieces of plastic top hats filled with gumballs. Winnie caught my eye and winked. Her purple and pink dress, into which she was squeezed like a holiday sausage, was a sight to behold.

"I've hired the best deejay in the city," Jimbo continued, pointing to a fat man with a pompadour sorting through CDs. "I want the champagne to flow like a river. This is it, ladies, my ticket to Celebration, Florida." He fingered his bow tie. "Anybody know how to tie this thing?" he asked. Peggy stepped forward, reaching out with golden fingernails.

All night, I was in a funk. I kept forgetting drink orders, forgetting to act glamorous. When I dropped a tray of appletinis, Jimbo grabbed me firmly by the elbow and hauled me into his office.

"Caroline, have I made myself clear?" he said.

"I'm sorry," I said.

"Are you drunk?"

I was, but just a little. "No," I said.

"Please," said Jimbo. "Whatever it is that's bothering you, please put it out of your mind, just for a few hours."

"I will." Jimbo stood before me, twisting his hands. He made me so sad suddenly: his thinning hair, his curled fingers. He had been running The Highball for thirty years. Jimbo's wife had been a jazz singer. She drank herself to death by forty.

I moved a box of mint julep glasses and sat down. Jimbo's office was filled with relics from the old days: pictures of Sinatra at The Highball, dusty Mardi Gras beads. "I just need a minute," I told Jimbo.

"OK, OK, but in ten I want you back on the floor."

"I promise."

"Don't let me down, Caroline," he said.

I took a few deep breaths, then fluffed my feathers and headed out. I couldn't stop thinking about everyone's sadnesses: my mother's forced cheer; my father's bloody death; Anthony, looking to me for hope. I thought of my mother, bringing us to church when we were small. "Pray for help," she told us, and we did. We prayed and we prayed, but no help came. Maybe Madeline was right: I was still waiting.

Crystal Robbins arrived late, her boyfriend on her arm. The deejay was well into his Wham! medley, and three drunk podiatrists were jamming to "Wake Me Up Before You Go Go." Crystal had a group of angular friends with her.

"Supermodels," whispered Peggy. "Look, there's Anita!" They stood at the doorway, taking in the scene. "The one with the pasties is Crystal," said Peggy. Crystal's boyfriend wore leather pants and a shirt unbuttoned to his navel. His hair was long and greasy-looking, and he was unshaven. He and most of the models wore sunglasses with yellow lenses. As the women headed toward a table in my section, the boyfriend walked around, inspecting the view, the carpet, the giant motor that kept us spinning.

I cleared my throat and marched over to the supermodels. "Welcome to The Highball!" I said, with as much merriment as I could muster.

"What a dump," one of them said. "Is the DJ actually George Michael?"

"We have lots of wonderful drink specials," I announced, "and you'll surely be delighted by our holiday appetizer platter."

"Huh?" said one of the girls, sliding her sunglasses down her slim nose and peering over them.

"Can we get a bottle of Ketel One?" asked the one named Anita.

"And, like, an ashtray?" another added.

"No problem," I said. I turned, but one of the girls caught my sleeve.

"Hey," she said, "is this Ungaro?" I shrugged. "It totally is! Leticia wore this in the *Bazaar* shoot."

I smiled, hoping to be included in more supermodel conversation. "Bottle of Ketel One?" Anita reminded me.

"Oh," I said, "sorry."

Winnie stood behind the bar. Her rings caught the light and sent sparkling circles to the walls. "I'm ready, Big Bird," she said. "Lay it on me. What do supermodels drink?"

"Vodka," I said.

"On the rocks?"

"Nope," I said, "they just want the bottle."

"Oh Lord," said Winnie. She pulled out a bottle of Absolut.

"Ketel One," I said.

"No."

"Yeah. They asked for it specifically."

"Shit. The footsie doctors drank it all." She pointed to the dance floor, where two women sang along to "I Want Your Sex," their vodka tonics held high.

"Call Kit," I said.

"No can do," she said. "He was drunk at noon."

"Len?" I suggested. I found Peggy, and explained the situation. She ran to the bar and picked up the phone. She dialed, held it to her ear, and then said, "Hello?" I saw Jimbo watching the models from the door of his office. His hands were clasped, as if in prayer. The boyfriend was still wandering around, fondling fixtures. "This is his fiancée! Who the hell is *this*?" said Peggy, her voice rising.

Winnie closed her eyes.

"Get an empty Ketel One bottle," I told Winnie, "and fill it with cold vodka. Hurry."

"Hey!" called one of the supermodels. "We gonna get some drinks before next year?" They erupted into laughter. I went over with an appetizer platter.

"Hi," I said. "Our bartender's just getting your vodka from cold storage. In the meantime, please enjoy these, compliments of the house."

"Is this a Chee-to?" said Anita, holding up the orange tidbit.

"Why is that stripper crying?" asked Crystal. I turned, and there was Peggy, collapsed against the bar, sobbing.

"Her boyfriend cheated on her," I said.

"Bastard!" said Crystal, and then she looked up quickly to make sure Mr. Leather Pants was within eyeshot.

"Tell her to come over here," said Anita, stuffing Cheetos in her mouth.

Just then, Winnie arrived, brandishing a bottle in an ice bucket. "Hey, girls," she said. "Here's your vodka."

"Didn't we ask for two bottles?" said a supermodel with an unidentifiable accent.

By the end of the night, we were pouring gin into Ketel One bottles and they were drinking it. The podiatrist crew was sloshed, the deejay was full into a Michael Jackson retrospective, and Peggy had lost a fiancé but gained a new posse of supermodel girlfriends. Peggy, Winnie, and I toasted the New Year with cheap champagne we had poured into empty Veuve Cliquot bottles, and then Jimbo called us into his office.

"Ladies," he said, "I have good news and bad news." He smiled at us kindly. Somehow a feather had gotten lodged in my mouth, and I was trying to get it out. "The Highball has been sold at last," he said. "Mr. Ponds plans to turn it into a hip nightspot. It will be called Cloud 8." He raised his eyebrows at this, as if to say, *what do I know.*

"Cheers!" said Peggy, holding up a glass.

"Cheers!" Winnie and I said. We all clinked glasses.

"Unfortunately," continued Jimbo, "the bar will stop revolving."

"That's terrible," I said.

"Uh," said Jimbo, "and that's not all."

We looked at him, the sweet old man who had taken care of us for years. "Uh," said Jimbo, and then he said that Cloud 8 would be staffed by models. "You know, um, young girls for the young crowd. Uh." He gave us an attempt at a smile.

"What are you saying?" said Winnie.

"Uh," said Jimbo again, and then he explained that what he was saying is that we were fired.

Bobby's Bar stayed open until dawn for us. I stumbled home, half my feathers lost along the way, and I fell into bed. My answering machine blinked madly, but I closed my eyes before playing the messages. The phone rang while I tossed and turned, and though I knew something must be wrong, I did not answer it.

It was not until the next afternoon that I found out my mother was dead.

PART TWO

ONE

FOR A TIME, there was so much to do that I did not think about what my life would be like without my mother. In a strange way, it felt good to say, *my mother died.* And: *my mother was in an accident.* I would speak the words gravely, with a shake of my head, and wait for the shocked response, the outpouring of sympathy. I didn't understand, you see. It was all a big new thing, a reason for getting on with every day. I had no job, now, no lover, no fucking life. My mother was dead. It was something.

I went back to New York. Still, it was like she was on a vacation. Her condo was the same. It was filled with her friends, with cocktail conversation. A Christmas party in January. There was the funeral, a closed casket. Madeline, despite feeling tired from her pregnancy, handled all the details. I drank and listened to my mother's friends talk about the things that kept them rooted to the world: their children, their jobs. Now there were grandchildren to talk about, and retirement plans. None of my mother's friends seemed to think about what was underneath the surface of their lives: did the years add up to something that made them proud? Were they satisfied, at peace? Had my mother been happy, I wanted to know. Had she been happy in her life?

It was a terrible accident. What else could you say? She was driving home from the Cherokee Club, after the New Year's Eve Ball. She had surely been drinking, and yet the accident was not her fault. It was a teenager from Port Chester, an outsider. *What had he even been doing in Holt?* people wondered, though Port Chester was only a few minutes away. But he wasn't one of us. He wasn't drunk. He was seventeen, and he wasn't paying attention. He didn't stop at the red light on Woodland Road. He drove right on through, hit my mother's Mercedes going forty. You wouldn't think forty could kill anyone.

She lived a good life. She loved you girls. She lived every day to the fullest. She's up in heaven, waiting for you. She's with your father. Maybe Ellie's with them. She's watching you. She was so proud.

Was she proud? Not of me. When I played piano for long afternoons, she'd stand at the doorway of the living room, lean her head to one side, and close her eyes. She was filled with pride when I was accepted to Juilliard, but was baffled that I decided to go to New Orleans instead.

Maybe I had made the wrong decisions in my life. At my mother's funeral, I wished I could go back in time. I could have been a famous pianist, or at least played a few songs on occasion. I could have made my mother proud; it wouldn't have taken much.

I slept forever. I lay in my mother's double bed and stared at the ceiling. Madeline came and went, brought me tea and toast, gave me Xanax, half a tablet at a time. One day—a week had passed, or almost a week—she sat next to me on the bed, her knees pulled into her chest. "What are we going to do?" she asked.

"I don't know," I said.

"I mean, about the condo. About..." she gestured with both hands, splaying them open. "All this stuff," she said.

"I lost my job," I said. Of course, I could have worked for the last month of The Highball, but it seemed pointless now.

"Yeah."

"Did I already tell you?"

"Yes."

"Oh."

"So what are you saying?" said Madeline. "You want to live here?" She looked around my mother's bedroom. When my father died, my mother tried to keep the big house up, but soon tired of dealing with the lawnmower and empty rooms. I could still remember the hope in her voice when she called to tell me about the condo. "If I sit up in bed," she'd said, "I can look out at the sea!" But a view of the water was her dream, not mine.

"No," I said, "that's not what I'm saying."

"Should we sell it?"

"I guess so. Yes."

You had to be impressed with Madeline's organizational skills. A few hazy days after our conversation, a frenetic woman named Irene began "popping by" to show the condo to potential buyers. I could hear her, pushing into my mother's closets, her bedroom, talking about remodeling options, about promise. Couples–some my age–trailed behind her. They asked if we had rodent problems (no), if we were including appliances in the purchase price (yes). I thought about stopping the whole process, but I wasn't going to stay in Holt, and neither was Madeline, who loved city life. We talked to the lawyer; my mother left us everything. We were all she had, and it made me so very sad that I had not really understood that, had not tried to make more of myself.

Madeline and I picked rooms and went to work. Madeline packed my mother's beautiful clothes into boxes. I took a pair of yellow high heels that I had seen her wear on special occasions. Madeline took a Chanel suit.

I tackled my mother's desk, which she had used to store papers and photographs. The desk had a large wooden panel that folded down for writing, and many small drawers and cubbyholes. Every little space was crammed full. I made a cup of tea and settled on the floor. In one compartment, there were dozens of my mother's manila folders. Each, I knew, represented a dead-end.

I paged through the typewritten reports. My mother had tracked down everyone we had ever known, it seemed: there were reports on her family members, my father's old girlfriends, and parents of our childhood friends. She had saved everything, and I imagined she'd drunk spritzers at night and re-read these papers, hoping to see something she had missed before.

She hounded people, year after year. And though she had shown me pictures of women who looked vaguely like Ellie, the *People Magazine* picture was the first one that made my heart beat fast.

After flipping through the papers for a while, I sighed and rubbed my eyes. I put the Ellie folders in a pile and stuck them back in the desk. I wasn't ready to throw them away.

From other compartments in my mother's desk, I emptied handfuls of family photographs. There we were, all three girls dressed the same, playing on the lawn, sprawling in the hammock. There was my mother in a bikini, a tiny Madeline resting on her hip.

Even earlier: pictures of my mother as a Savannah debutante, her hair short and framing her head like a cap: the pixie cut. There were photographs of my grandparents: my grandmother relaxing on a chaise in the sunlight; my grandfather smiling, leaning against a splintered wooden door at their house on the Vernon River. I had heard about the river house. It was part of the blissful life *before.* My mother talked often of *before*, the dreamy days *before* she married my father. Afternoons spent crabbing, the smell of the river. My mother ditched her fiancé and ran off to New York when she was eighteen. She knew she was destined for more, she told me, and Manhattan represented freedom. She met my father on a blind date when she was twenty, and felt like a movie star on his arm. She married him, ending the glorious days *before.*

*

Madeline had gone to the Container Store and bought wooden boxes for photographs. Maybe she thought her baby would want to look through these, dive into these jumbled memories. And though I didn't even have a boyfriend, much less a hope of a family, I began to cry when I realized that if I ever did have a child, it would never know the smell of my mother's soft neck.

I piled the pictures in the boxes with little regard for order or theme. I started wondering what a stranger would think, happening upon these pictures. Could they pick, out of a group of young men and women at a party, which two would marry? I found my mother's engagement portrait, spent a while looking at her knowing smile.

Was my mother's faint unhappiness visible only to me, as she stood stiffly under the Christmas tree with my father? And Ellie: what would a stranger see in her faraway child's gaze?

Each wooden box had a square on the front cover, a place for an identifying photograph. I chose a picture of my mother, a teenage girl on a rickety dock, her feet in the water, chin thrust high.

My father didn't have many childhood pictures. He grew up on a farm in Ohio, where, he told us a hundred times, he had learned the value of a dollar. I stared for a long time at a picture of my father at five. He wore an oversized coat and looked forlornly at the camera.

I had long wondered why my parents had married. They were both good-looking, but could they really have thought that would be enough? I remembered being small and thinking my father ran the world. He always guided my mother, one strong hand in the small of her back. She would ask him how to cook things, how to dress.

When I was young, I waited for my father to come home each evening. He would hang his coat on the coat tree, place his briefcase on the floor. He would loosen his tie. I would hold out my hand, and he would take it. We had tea parties in my room or read books, but the first hour of the evening was for me. He would check in on baby Madeline, give my mother a dry kiss, but it was I who helped him shed his workaday demeanor, who made him laugh and sing songs from *Free to Be You and Me.*

I remember telling him stories, the way he would focus on me. He was so important to me that capturing his attention felt like the biggest prize. I suppose we all believed that my father could keep us safe. Maybe that's what love is, in the end: a shared illusion of safety.

I found my mother's love letters from various boys, saved as ammunition against my father, as private comfort. I read a few, but they all started to sound the same: *Dearest Isabelle; beautiful Isabelle; missing you, Isabelle.* It took me hours to comb through the contents of the desk. By dinnertime, I was finished, a neat stack of boxes ready for the closet.

"Done?" I looked up, and Ron was standing in the doorway to my mother's bedroom.

"Yeah," I said, standing and stretching my arms.

"Want to come to the Grill for dinner?"

"Well," I said, thinking of being alone, of watching television and ordering a pizza. "I think I might just stay here."

"Would it bother you if we went into the city? I think Maddy could use some time away...."

"Of course," I said.

"You'll be OK?"

I nodded. "I've got a good book," I lied.

"Really?" he said. "What?"

"I can't remember...something about...Egypt."

"Oh. That sounds interesting."

"Yeah," I said.

The condo was quiet without them, and without my mother. I opened a bottle of her pinot grigio and turned on the TV, switching channels for a while. Finally, I went back upstairs to her bedroom and lay on my mother's bed, which still smelled of her. I pressed my nose to her pillowcase, and fell asleep.

TWO

I DREAMT OF MY MOTHER at eighteen years old: Isabelle Bonnot. She was bones in a bathing suit, sitting on the edge of a dock. Her hair was long and salty, her eyes clear brown. It was August in Savannah. The heat was overwhelming, and she moved her feet slowly through the water.

The air smelled of the river: marshy and thick. The river stretched past their house, which was white, and completely surrounded by a screen porch. Ten wide steps spanned the space between the lawn and the porch door. Isabelle's father said that he always knew when she was coming. "She makes an entrance," he would say, "ten thuds and one big slam from that goddamned door." The door was thirty years old, and cracked from the heat, but Isabelle's mother wouldn't let anyone replace it.

There was a wooden swing hanging from a tree to the right of the house. The family called it the Lovers' Swing because it was where almost every marriage proposal in the family had occurred. Isabelle was the most recent; her beau, Bernard, had asked for her hand at the beginning of the summer, and they were due to be married in the fall. Isabelle's engagement portrait had arrived from the photographer, and tonight she would give a copy to Bernard.

Isabelle started when she heard a cry. Aunt Betty was visible over the water: a wide straw hat, a brown arm held high, a flash of pink lips. "Here I come!" she yelled. She was floating on her back from her house to theirs. The Vernon River ran past all Isabelle's relatives' houses. Next door was her grandmother's, then the house that had been bought up by a Yankee outsider, and then the house where Aunt Betty lived.

The current carried Aunt Betty steadily closer, and Isabelle could make out the gin and tonic in her hand. "Isabelle, sweetie!" said Aunt Betty, "get ready to grab my drink!"

It was a humid Sunday night, a white rum night, as Isabelle's mother called it, though there were bottles of every sort lined up on the porch bar. Sunday clambakes always began with Betty floating down the river from her dock to the Bonnots', and when the current changed, around midnight, she floated home and another week began. Betty's arm was strong; Isabelle pulled her from the water. "Well!" said Betty, smoothing the skirt of her bikini bottom. Her stomach was soft and brown, and her toenails were painted. "Give me that drink, sweetie," she said, "and while you're at it, go tell your mama to mix me a fresh one."

"Yes'm," said Isabelle, and she ran down the dock over the lawn to the porch, where her mother lay on her chaise. "Mama?"

Isabelle's mother opened her eyes. "Hi love," she said. "Aunt Betty here?" Isabelle nodded. "Wants a drink?"

"I'll mix it," said Isabelle, "don't get up, now."

"You're my angel from heaven." Isabelle's mother closed her

eyes. "Take a shower, after," she said.

Isabelle made the drink, and then went up the stairs to her bedroom. Each step creaked underneath her. The setting sun shone straight in her window, and she sat on her bed. Her room had been her mother's, once. The canopies over the twin beds had faded, but were still a rich yellow that matched the cotton bedcovers.

The night before, when Isabelle's mother came to kiss her goodnight, Isabelle said, "Mama, I'm not sure I want to get married yet."

Isabelle's mother sat on the bed. Her hair was tucked behind her ears, and the smell of her lotion made Isabelle's stomach relax. "Bernard's a sweet boy."

"But what if he's not my one true love?"

Isabelle's mother smoothed her hair. "Roll over for a scratch," she said. Her nails were cool and wonderful on Isabelle's back.

"I know how you feel," said Isabelle's mother. "I almost didn't marry your daddy," she said, and then she laughed. "I had all sorts of dreams and plans." The room was quiet, and the scratching stopped.

"Like what?" said Isabelle, rolling over and looking up at her mother.

"Like...." She looked out the window, where the stars were blocked by clouds. She put her hands to her eyes, and then took them away.

"Isabelle," she said, "I was a good daughter to my mama. I've been a good wife to your daddy, and a good mama to you and your sister." She smiled and raised her eyebrows. "Now what could be more important?" she said.

"Nothing," said Isabelle, though the sick feeling had come back.

"Life is not always just right and just perfect," said Isabelle's mother. "But you don't give up and you push on. You put some dreams in a drawer." White light moved across her face, and the sound of Isabelle's father's car came close. Her stare was blank, and Isabelle felt scared.

"Now that's your daddy home," said Isabelle's mother, and she kissed Isabelle and stood up. Her bathrobe trailed behind her as she left.

After showering, Isabelle changed into a pink dress and applied her mother's lavender lotion. She slid her engagement photo from its envelope. In the picture, she looked beautiful. Her hair was pulled into combs, and she wore the pearls Bernard had given her the night before the photo shoot. The photographer had done something to the background of the portrait: everything looked hazy except for Isabelle's face, which was clear and lovely. Even her shoulders were blurred; it looked as if she were rising from smoke. In the portrait, she stared at the camera, a half-smile on her face. She looked confident, adult. She looked as if she knew what she was doing.

Bernard arrived with his hair still wet, his cheeks red from a day spent fishing. Isabelle held the portrait as she watched Bernard give her mother a bunch of irises. He wore a pale pink shirt and pressed khaki shorts. His eyes sparkled with mischief. Ever since childhood, he had been up to something. Isabelle remembered the time he hid a frog in her bed, and the time he pretended she had a twig in her hair and leaned in close, surprising her with a kiss.

When she looked at him—the confident way he crossed his arms over his chest and leaned back, listening to Isabelle's father—she could see the boy inside him.

The moon rose, round and light. Glass and silverware and jewelry flashed in the candlelight. The heat did not thin, and perspiration made Isabelle's family's faces shine at the edges. Her mother lifted her hair to reveal damp skin underneath, and her father rolled up the sleeves of his shirt, shaking his head at the heat, the one situation he could not fix. Bernard brought the electric fan out, pulling it as far as its cord would stretch, and everyone turned toward its breeze in mid-sentence as it passed over them.

"We can move inside," said Isabelle's mother, more than once, but no one could bear to leave the moonlight and the clicking of crickets. The river ran nearby, its currents catching the light like a mirror.

Bernard poured from his flask into Isabelle's lemonade, and the edges of her vision grew slippery. Bernard's lips were warm on her shoulder blades and her neck. Isabelle's mother put out the crab, baskets full, and the lemons and butter. They cracked the salty bodies and left the empty shells in large clay bowls. "There will be no ceremony here!" said Isabelle's father, and he set the precedent of ignoring the tiny forks and silver crackers. He sucked the meat from his crabs, and the butter ran down his wrists and made his lips shine.

Isabelle ate five crabs, and six buttered slices of corn bread. She filled a bowl with grapes, and sat on the Lovers' Swing. Next to her, Bernard fed her grapes, the cool juice mixing with the salty crab on his fingertips. "Do you love me?" she asked

Bernard, and he said, "Of course, darlin'. What's not to love?"

It was late when Bernard asked Isabelle to walk down by the dock. They spent evenings there, on a blanket they kept folded on the crabbing boat. Every week, Isabelle tried to wash the blanket with the hose behind the house, rubbing soap into it and hanging it to dry in the sun. It had grown brittle and rough, and it smelled faintly of fish, marshy water, and soap. Isabelle hated the smell. She wished they could lie in a featherbed, with clean, soft sheets. They spread the blanket on the dock, and the waves rocked them and they talked and did not have sex. Bernard had stopped asking, but his kisses were probing. Isabelle could feel the wooden boards underneath her hipbones when she lay on her side to look up at Bernard, and she could hear the splashes of fish and bugs nearing the surface of the river.

Most everyone had gone home. This time of the night—too late for adults—belonged to Isabelle and Bernard. They lay on the lawn and planned their life. Bernard wanted five children to fill his family's brownstone in Savannah. He talked about coming home from work and taking his family for evening strolls around the city to look at the azaleas. "We'll get you help with the cooking," he told Isabelle, "but you're going to have to mix my drinks."

The story of their future pleased Bernard, and he twirled Isabelle's hair around his finger as he talked. But increasingly, Isabelle had begun to wonder about other lives she could lead: painting landscapes in Paris, or being a fashion model in New York City. She felt panicked at the thought of staying in Savannah forever, and becoming a woman just like her mother.

Isabelle told Bernard to wait a minute, and she fetched the portrait. She went into the bathroom to put a drop of perfume behind each ear: a surprise for Bernard when he kissed her there. She looked into the mirror and saw that her cheeks were flushed. She did not want to leave the bathroom.

Isabelle looked at her portrait. This girl hasn't even lived, *she thought.* She doesn't know a thing.

Isabelle's mother always talked about the same memories, as if only a few instants burned themselves into her mind. Isabelle didn't know it, but this would be one of the moments she would come back to again and again when she tried to make sense of her life. The portrait would always remind her of a night full of moonlight and Bernard's mouth and the smell of the river. The night when she decided to run away to New York, thinking she deserved better than what she had.

When Isabelle handed him the photo, Bernard took each of her hands and kissed them. He pulled the picture out and took a long look. "Oh my," he said. He pulled Isabelle close and kissed her hair. "My beautiful girl," he said.

"I'm not a girl, you know," said Isabelle. Bernard kissed her neck and her collarbones.

"Be quiet, doll," he said. And Isabelle was quiet. It was time to leave, to shed the old Isabelle like a cocoon. Bernard put his arms around her. They lay on the blanket and the heat came up in waves from the river.

When Bernard was asleep, Isabelle stole into the house. She filled her suitcase with clothes. She took all her money and most of her shoes. She did not know that she would meet the wrong man, and marry him. She did not know that she would have three daughters, and lose one. She was filled with hope and purpose. She knew that she had to leave her home to find herself.

The bus station was two miles away. As she walked, she pretended she was there already, at the top of the Empire State Building, a cigarette in her fingers, the lights of Manhattan spread before her like stars.

THREE

When I woke, the knowledge fell into my head like a stone. I was going to Montana. Like my mother, I needed to see what the world held in store for me. And if Ellie was alive, I was going to find her.

I headed into the city to tell my sister. Ron and Madeline lived on East 64th Street. It was still freezing cold in New York. Walking uptown from Grand Central, I bought a Kangol hat for ten bucks, and eyed a faux-alligator purse. "Fifteen dollars," said a beautiful black man.

"Fifteen dollars?" I said.

He gave me a wide smile. "Thirteen dollars?"

"Deal," I said. As I rummaged in my pocket, he opened a box.

"Label?" he asked.

I deliberated between Gucci and Hermès, but went for Kate Spade. He took out a glue gun and pressed the label on. "Where are you from?" I asked.

"Ghana."

"Wow," I said, "how'd you get here?"

"I fly, lady," said the man, who was clearly finished with me.

So much for love in the afternoon. I kept walking.

Ron opened the door to the apartment. "Hey," he said, "It's Caroline from the 'hood."

"What?" I said.

"Your hat," he said. "Kangol, very ghetto."

"Oh," I said, patting my head. "Well, I bought it up here, actually."

"They're the rage with the Spence and Nightingale girls," said Ron.

"Anyway," I said, "can I come in?"

Ron stepped aside, and I took in the huge living room. High ceilings, pale blue walls, velvet couch big enough to live in. "It's beautiful," I said. Madeline had a gorgeous piano, though she didn't play, and on the piano there were two pictures in silver frames. One was Madeline and Ron on their wedding day. Madeline smiled widely, and Ron looked shell-shocked. The other picture was taken on Christmas, many years ago. Under a big tree, the three Winters girls hugged each other.

"Maddy's drying her hair," said Ron. "You want some green tea?"

"Oh, come on," I said. He shrugged, pointed toward the bedroom with his thumb.

"It's good for you," he said.

"How about a Bloody Mary?"

"Coming up."

Madeline came into the room, her hair swept up and sprayed into place. Her face seemed rounder, and her stomach swelled just the smallest bit. But she looked tired, and her eyes were red, as if she had been up late, or crying. She was affixing an enormous diamond to her ear.

"Hi," I said, "you look wonderful." She leaned forward and kissed the air above my head.

"Hey," she said, "what do you want?"

"Wow," I said.

"Well, are you here for tea?"

"I just need some snowpants," I said.

"Snowpants?"

"Yes," I said.

"May I ask why you'll need snowpants in New Orleans?"

I took a breath. "I'm going to Montana," I said, "actually."

"Montana? I've always wanted to go there," said Ron, handing me a drink. "Good for you, Caroline."

"Ron, honey?" said Madeline in a steely voice. "Could you excuse us for a moment?"

"Let her be, Maddy," said Ron.

"You have no idea what's going on here," said Madeline.

Ron looked at me, and I nodded. "She's right," I said, "you don't."

"Fine," said Ron. He went down a hallway and I heard a door slam shut.

Madeline sank into her fabulous couch. "We're having problems," she said.

"I'm sorry," I said. "I'm sure you'll work them out."

"Montana, hey?" said Madeline.

"Yeah."

She shook her head. "I know why you're going," she said. She looked at me. "You think Mom wasn't begging me to go?"

"The picture does look like her, don't you think?" I sat down next to Madeline. As I expected, the couch was heavenly.

"It's a girl. She's the right age," said Madeline.

"The smile, though. Don't you remember Ellie's smile?"

"I think you're living in a dream world," said Madeline.

"It could be her," I said, "you don't know." I sounded petulant.

"Go the fuck to Montana," said Madeline. "What do I care? But when you need some help dealing with reality, I might be too damn tired." She blinked several times. "I guess it's the hormones," she said, "but things feel all mixed up."

She looked like she was about to cry. I sat there awkwardly. Madcline said, "It's my fault."

"What are you talking about?" I said.

Madeline sat back and looked me in the eye. "Ellie told me she was afraid," said Madeline. "She thought something bad was going to happen."

"What?"

"It was the night before we were going to run away. I was asleep. Shc was shaking me, crying from a nightmare."

"Ellie was crying?"

Madeline took a ragged breath. "She was hysterical. She

said…she had dreamed about shadows. About someone….” Madeline shook her head. “I was half asleep. I wasn't listening to her! It was something about Blind Brook. Shadows in Blind Brook.”

I sipped my Bloody Mary. I wasn't sure what to say. We all thought Ellie's disappearance was our fault, it seemed. My mother's obsessive search, my New Orleans vigil. And here was Madeline's private torment: dreams about Blind Brook.

“Did you tell the police?” I asked, finally.

“Yes. They said it was nothing.” Madeline gripped my hand. “I rolled over,” she said. “I told her we'd talk about it in the morning. She wanted to sleep with me, but I said no. She said she was scared….”

“We were kids,” I said. “Kids just say things, Maddy.”

“But then…,” said Madeline.

I finished it for her. “Then she was gone,” I said.

FOUR

"*Be Your Own Private Dick*?" yowled Winnie. "Now that's a book I could use!" She sipped her Budweiser. It was still light outside, yet here we were at Bobby's Bar. I had flown back to New Orleans to get ready for my trip.

"It means Private Investigator," I said.

"I know," said Winnie. "I'm just playing you."

"Oh," I said.

"So you're going to put all these private investigator books in that beat-up car of yours and drive to Montana?"

"Basically."

Winnie drained the rest of her can. The jukebox was loud: *Gonna kiss you where I miss you*.... "So what are you going to do when you get there?"

I shrugged.

"Good plan," said Winnie.

"Well, what are you doing next week?" I said. "Why don't you come with me?" Winnie ran her palms along the thighs of her red skirt. "You think I'm leaving that man alone?"

said Winnie, jerking her thumb at Kit, who appeared to be dancing with a metal chair.

"Someone would steal him?"

"You don't think so?" said Winnie. She sighed. "Well anyway," she said, "I'm getting my nails rhinestoned."

Winnie and I pored over a gas station map, anchoring it on four sides by beer cans. "Texas, New Mexico, Colorado, Wyoming, Montana," said Winnie incredulously. She took a long swig of her beer. "I've never been anywhere," she said. "Well, Mississippi."

Later, we talked about the chances that I'd pick up a hitchhiker like Brad Pitt. "Or maybe you'll fall in love with a cowboy," said Winnie.

"Or a cowpoke," I said.

"What's a cowpoke?" Her voice was blurred from the beer and whiskey.

"I don't know," I said. We dissolved into laughter.

"Sounds dirty," said Winnie. "Damn!"

By the time I realized I'd spend more than a plane ticket on gas to Montana, I was already committed to the idea of a road trip. I don't know what I hoped I'd find out there in the mountains, but as I drove drunk home from Bobby's, almost hitting a woman as I turned into my driveway, I hoped I'd find something more than what I had.

On my bedside table, I had a pile of books from the library. I sat in bed that night, and read a book about Patty Hearst and the Stockholm Syndrome, which occurred when an abducted person stopped believing he or she was abducted and started believing what their kidnapper told them was true. It was often less painful than understanding the real situation, the book said. If your real story was too terrible, the book said, you made a new one for yourself. Then you willed yourself to believe it.

I couldn't sleep, and watched the shadows on my wall as cars drove by. Outside, someone yelled, "You stabbed me! You stabbed me!" I realized that instead of being an out-of-work cocktail waitress with a murdered sister, no parents, and cellulite, I was going to Montana, trying to find a new story of my own.

FIVE

from the desk of

AGNES FOWLER

Dear Johan,

I have not heard back from you, but I gather the mail service might be very slow. It's a clear night here in Montana, but winter is in the air. I suppose I should enclose the Alaska Hunks.com Personality Plus! Profile. OK, I will.

Looking forward to hearing from you,

Agnes

ALASKAHUNKS.COM
PERSONALITY PLUS! PROFILE

1. Fave color

Hm. This should be an easy question, shouldn't it? But I've never known what my favorite color was. I used to say "purple," but I think I was trying to be exciting. I do like the deep green color of my living room. After my father died, I went to Kmart and bought cans of paint. I believe it was the Martha Stewart line. Let me find the color, might as well do this right. Hold on. It's IVY AFTERNOON. I'll go with that.

2. Fave music

Oh, dear. Where is "fave book," I'd like to know? (It's *Madame Bovary,* by the way.) Don't Alaskan Hunks care about books? I listen to moody pop music, like Phil Collins on a station called "Kiss 95." I like songs about love ending, though I hope that doesn't make me sound morbid. I'm all for show tunes, as well, like *Anything Goes.*

3. Fave sport

Is reading a sport?

4. Fave hobby

I wasn't really allowed to get out very much, so I tended to take up my father's hobbies, like making flies for fly-fishing. I also enjoy step aerobics and salsa dancing, though it's tough to find a spicy salsa partner in northwestern Montana.

5. *Fave smell*

What? This is a very strange question. Am I supposed to say I like the smell of new snow? I do. Also: tacos, gasoline, and soap.

6. *Fave food*

I do love food. Besides blueberry pancakes and various penny candy, I love shrimp scampi. Also, Entenmann's Raspberry Twist coffee cake.

7. *My motto*

"I can help any library patron!"

8. *My worst nightmare*

I'm going to skip this question.

9. *My greatest hope*

Sometimes, I wake before the sun has come up, and I feel that I am all alone in this world. I would like to not feel that way anymore.

10. *My perfect date*

Oh! This is the best question. First of all, I would be just the slightest bit sunburned. I love taking a shower and getting ready when my skin is a little—but not too—pink. I would use expensive shampoo, conditioner, and lotion. I actually have a Burt's Bees Sampler Pack with all sorts of creams and lotions that I got from my Secret Santa at the library. It's my perfect date! I'd use them all.

I would wear a beautiful shimmery skirt and a cream-colored wool sweater. (Or cotton, depending on the weather.) I would wear my mother's necklace, which would be cool on my sunburned neck.

Depending on the weather, I would wear sandals or snug boots.

My date will arrive smelling good, like pine trees. He will bring me flowers or a snack. I put the flowers (or snack) away, and we steal into the night. I roll down the window of his car (or sleigh) and feel cold air on my sunburned cheeks.

We go to dinner somewhere candle-lit and lovely. Across the table, he gazes at me. We talk about what books we have been reading and about how great we look. We eat lobsters.

After dinner, we're in a bed with silk sheets. He has slipped me out of my clothes, and now it's just me and my expensive lotion. He runs his ~~hands~~ tongue over my breasts and then my inner thighs.

Wait one minute while I refill my Chardonnay. . . .

He has oils on his fingers, and he runs them along my skin. (Though still his tongue is running over my breasts and inner thighs.) He kisses me and he smells of safety and he tastes like butter from the lobsters but NOT like lobsters, which are delicious but not sexy. Maybe we had some chocolate mousse for dessert, so he can taste like that.

He is skinny but strong. Not too much hair, esp. not on his back. He takes off his shirt and pants and socks. (Though still his tongue is running over my breasts and inner thighs.) Now he is moving inside me and saying my name again and again.

I am hot and wet and the sunburn makes my skin warm but I'm not so sunburned that I hurt at all. I don't hurt at all. Inside me, he moves back and forth and back and forth and I say his name, too. This goes on. When we climax, we do it together, or if not together, then nearly at the same time, that's OK. Then we lie in the silk sheets and fall asleep.

When I wake up, the sun is still not out, just the moon. But I am not alone.

SIX

When Isabelle took the bus to New York and left him, Bernard thought it was the end of the world. He awoke every morning, and for just an instant, he thought of her: her soapy smell, and the way she touched his ear with her lips. Her breath, which smelled like the toffee candies she carried with her everywhere. Her tongue, warm caramel in his mouth.

But then it descended, like a curtain closing out a colorful stage. She was gone. She left him a vague letter and all the presents he had ever given her, sealed up in a shoebox. I feel that I am destined for bigger things. I will carry you in my heart always. You will find someone who will love you the way you deserve to be loved.

Clichés, one after another, and now his mother's sapphire ring was back in the vault. Isabelle married a Yankee, he heard. Hadn't even come home for the wedding.

"Black coffee," said Bernard, looking at his watch. He was late again, not that anyone would say a word about it. His enormous

mahogany desk, shining, empty of any real work. The solicitous smirks of his father's employees as they passed his office, trying hard not to covet his picture windows, his grandfather clock.

"Black coffee, please,*" said the girl behind the counter. Bernard looked up at the blond girl, who offered him a smile. It was a flirtatious smile, and Bernard felt his neck growing hot. His tie was too tight.*

"Sorry," he said. "And a blueberry muffin. Please."

She was too young for him. Her hair was braided in two pigtails, like a blond Pocahontas. Her voice was pure Yankee, a little too loud, sharp. "Toasted?" she said, and Bernard nodded. He watched her movements, which were quick and decisive. She sliced the muffin in one stroke of a large knife, and slipped it on a metal tray, opening the oven door at the same time. Underneath the apron, she wore a tank top and men's pants. She was tan, with freckles across her shoulders.

"It's gonna be a minute," she said, putting her hands on her hips. Bernard nodded, and she cocked her head. "You can wait right over there," she said.

"Sorry," said Bernard. "I'm sorry."

"Don't be sorry," said the girl.

He waited for his muffin. It was not in his nature to wait. Usually, his secretary fetched his breakfast, or he skipped the meal altogether, waiting until afternoon to eat anything. Maybe he'd take this brazen girl to lunch, Bernard thought. She might enjoy The Oglethorpe Club, its sunny garden room.

He felt a stirring, and it took him a while to place it. Desire. He'd been with ladies, of course, but nothing like this, not since

Isabelle. He had lovers now, but he did not have someone to love.

"Black coffee, blueberry muffin!" the girl's voice rang out over the sipping and the toasting and the steaming and the foot-steps of people outside. Bernard walked to the counter, where the girl held a white paper bag, the top folded over cleanly.

He took the bag, and their fingers touched for a second too long. "Thank you," he said. Then he said it again: "Thank you."

The girl laughed. "I'm Sarah," she said.

"Sarah," repeated Bernard.

"Are you just going to stand there," said the girl, "or are you going to ask me out?"

"Please," said Bernard.

SEVEN

I SET OUT for Montana on Saturday. I had taken care of everything: my next-door neighbors would feed Georgette and water the plants, the car had new oil and a full tank of gas. I bought a road map of the United States, and a Polaroid camera (#3 on the Essentials List in *Be Your Own Private Dick*). I had filled a cooler with beer, Fresca, and Moon Pies.

It was strange, driving past the Tastee, CC's Coffee Shop, Whole Foods. I took a left at the enormous gardens that sheltered the art museum, feeding onto Carrolton (passing a sign that said FRESH SWIMP) and then I-10. I would be on I-10 until New Mexico, unless I took a detour for thrills. I turned on the radio, and Johnny Cash sang.

On the third day of my trip, I picked up the hitchhiker. She was a teenage girl, not a hunk. She stood by the side of the road in a denim miniskirt and T-shirt, a duffel bag at her feet. This was in a dusty town in northern New Mexico; I was searching for a spot to eat a late lunch. At about the same time that I saw the sign for "Manuel's Tacos Y Mas," I saw the girl. I slowed down.

The girl watched me steadily as I neared her. I rolled down my window. "Are you a hitchhiker?" I asked. She had curly hair, brown eyes, and a flat nose.

"Pretty much yes," she said.

"I'm going to have some lunch," I said. "And then I can drive you."

She looked at the ground. "Do you want something to eat?" I asked. She did not answer. But when I parked and went inside, the girl followed me, and slid into my booth.

When I said I'd have *huevos rancheros,* she said, "The same for me."

We ate chips and drank ice water from red plastic glasses. "What's your name?" I asked.

"Roxie."

"Where are you headed?"

She shrugged. Her shoulders were narrow, and I could see her bones through her T-shirt, which was worn thin as silk. She seemed gloomy. Her front teeth overlapped a bit, and this chipmunk-like attribute made her seem harmless. "I'm going to Montana," I said.

"Oh," said Roxie, "OK."

"Are you from around here?" I asked.

"Sure," she said. I looked out the window at the scrubby landscape. Heat shimmered in waves above the parched land. The restaurant smelled like hamburger. Suddenly, Roxie seemed to focus. She leaned toward me. "How about Denver?" she said.

"What?"

"You can take me to Denver?"

I blinked, thinking of the road north. "Yeah," I said, "I can take you to Denver."

"Denver," she said, nodding, as if making a decision. "Yes, Denver," she said, emphatically. She placed her hand on the table, palm down. She looked up at me happily.

"What's in Denver?" I asked.

"Everything," said the girl. "Everything is in Denver." I smiled. I was looking forward to getting there myself. The desert didn't turn me on. It was scary, hot, and desolate. But mountains I felt I could go for.

Our food came, and as we ate I watched the girl. For someone who had been hitchhiking, she did not seem particularly hungry. She ate with small, rabbitty bites, expertly scooping up the runny yolk and sauce with a hot tortilla from the round holder in the center of the table. She used enough hot sauce to kill a man. I did not use any.

I ordered a Coke to go, which seemed to confuse the waiter, a squat older fellow. Roxie translated in rapid Spanish, and the man brought me a Styrofoam coffee cup filled with Coke and covered by Saran Wrap. "To go," said Roxie, flicking her wrist in disdain. "We don't do that here."

As Roxie settled in the passenger seat of the Wagoneer, her duffel bag at her feet, I wondered what she had meant by "we." New Mexicans? Hispanic Americans? Had she meant she was from this little town ("Chama," it was called), or just that she was familiar with small Mexican restaurants? Was I taking Roxie away from her home? Roxie played with the radio, and landed us on a bouncy radio station where a man sang in Spanish.

"This is OK?" she asked, peering at me with those brown eyes.

"Um, sure," I said. I had never actually listened to one of the Spanish-language stations before. All the seesawing music sounded the same to me. But what was a hitchhiker for, if not to broaden your horizons? After all, I didn't like R&B until I started spending time at Bobby's Bar.

Roxie leaned back against the seat, closing her eyes and singing vaguely along with the radio. I tried to figure out how old she was: sixteen? Nineteen? She seemed old enough to have had some trouble, but not to have been beaten by it. After a time, she fell asleep. I drove north, into Colorado.

The mountains sliced into the sky. I followed the ribbon of road, clinging to the steering wheel for my life. Roxie's music really began to grate on me. The sun did not set slowly; it was in the sky, and then it was behind a mountain, leaving the road eerie and dim. I turned off the radio, and Roxie stirred. "What's happening?" she said irritably.

"I need to sleep," I said. The friendship I'd hoped would spring forth between me and Roxie, the confessions, the secrets revealed, none of it had come to pass. She was just a quiet girl who liked annoying music. I wanted to tell her—to tell someone—about my mother.

We were approaching Colorado Springs. On the map, it looked to be a sprawling city. I wasn't in the mood, so I pulled into the Sleepy Time Motel on the outskirts. "I can sleep right here," said Roxie, indicating the back seat of the Wagoneer.

I almost let her—after all, she could have been a serial killer, but then I said, "Oh please. Don't be a dope." I rented us a room with two big beds, both of which were bolted to the floor. We went across the street to Bob's Big Boy and ordered some burgers to go. I lugged the cooler, which still had plenty of Dixies, into our room. I was ready for HBO and a comfy bed.

Roxie ate her burger daintily, dabbing at the corners of her mouth with the yellow napkin. I pulled a Dixie from the cooler, which was no longer cool. I fished around for the bottle opener. "Damn," I muttered.

"What's the issue?" said Roxie.

"I think I forgot my bottle opener in my motel room in Texas," I said.

"No problemo," said Roxie. She held her slim fingers out for the beer, and I handed it to her. She lifted the bottle to her mouth, inserted it, and snapped the cap off with her teeth in a clean motion, then handed me the bottle and smiled sweetly. "I did this for my mother," she said.

"Thanks." I took a long sip, and then said, "My mother's dead."

Roxie looked at me steadily. "I'm sorry," she said.

"Me too," I said, and I felt tears in my throat.

"You miss her," said Roxie. I nodded. Roxie watched me sympathetically. Then she opened the cooler, pulled out a Dixie, and cracked it open between her molars. She set the second beer on the table between us. "Now one is waiting," she said.

We watched the television—an HBO special about pimps—

and I cried quietly. The world was so gray now, without my beautiful mom.

At the sight of Denver, its towering buildings and wide highways, Roxie seemed to balk. “What about Montana?” she said, when we stopped to get gas.

“Sorry?”

“What’s in Montana?” she said. “Your husband?”

“No,” I said, “my sister.”

“Is she a cowgirl?” asked Roxie.

“I’m not sure,” I said. “I don’t know who she is. She’s missing.”

Roxie raised her eyebrows. “Missing!” she said.

“Yup.”

She let this percolate while I went inside to pay for the gas and some gum. When I got back in the car, Roxie was looking at my map. “Well,” I said, “this is Denver. Here we are.”

“Oh no,” said Roxie. “Let’s go Montana.”

“Let’s go Montana?”

Roxie sighed, rolled her eyes. “Let’s go *to* Montana,” she said.

“Oh,” I said, turning the engine over, “OK.”

We drove in companionable silence, the road like a snake, the mountains jagged and awesome. When the last of the Spanish-language radio stations faded, Roxie propped her feet on the dashboard and turned to me. “How are you going to find the cowgirl?” she asked.

“You mean my sister?”

"Yes."

I didn't answer for a minute. "Well," I said, finally, "I have a picture of her. I'm going to show it around."

"Show it around?"

"Yeah, that's what I said."

"Can I see it?"

"Sure. I'll get it out at the next stop." Roxie nodded. She rolled down the window, closing her eyes and letting the cold air spill over her face. Finally, I asked her to put the window back up.

I pulled into the Teton Mart, and while the car was filling with gas, I rummaged through my bag. I took out the folder and opened it on the hood of the car. Roxie leaned in and peered at the photo. "Well, which one?" she said. I pointed to the smiling girl in the picture.

"Oh," said Roxie, visibly disturbed.

"What do you mean, *oh*?"

Roxie looked up at me, and shaded her eyes from the sun. Her hair blew around her face. "That girl is not missing," she said.

"She...she disappeared. When we were small. Everyone thinks she's dead...but that's her. It has to be." I sounded like a mess, even to myself. I sounded desperate.

Roxie looked again at the picture, traced her long fingernail along the side of Ellie's face. "That girl does not want to be found," said Roxie. She looked up. "I know," she said, "she's like me."

"What do you mean?"

"You know what I mean," said Roxie. It was true; I did.

"Can I have a Big Gulp?" said Roxie. I gave her a five, and she walked toward the log cabin store. The gas tank filled, and I unhooked the pump. I screwed the cap on, and then flicked the gas cover closed. I was holding the folder with trembling fingers.

I knew what I had to do. I took Roxie's duffel from the back seat, and I placed it on top of the gas pump. I got behind the steering wheel and started the car. I put the car in first.

It was not Roxie: she was a nice enough girl, who had problems of her own. It wasn't even Ellie, or the painful knowledge that surely awaited me. It wasn't me, or my mother. It was just loss, pure and simple. Loss–its heavy ache–made the tears run down my cheeks as I pulled out, leaving Roxie behind.

EIGHT

The Thunderbird Motel in Missoula, Montana, beckoned to me. It was crowned by an enormous pink sign. I pulled the Wagoneer into the parking lot and went in the door marked "Office." The man at the front desk looked like Elvis in his later, haggard years.

"All booked up," he said, not removing the cigarette from between his lips.

"Oh," I said. I looked around the lobby, taking in the coffeepot, the faded green chairs.

"Amway convention."

"Thanks," I said.

"You on your honeymoon?" he asked.

I turned back around. What about my unkempt appearance could have made him think I was well loved, satiated, and celebratory? "I'm sorry. Did you say *honeymoon*?"

He nodded, finally taking the stub from his mouth and dropping it in the metal ashtray on the counter. "Reason is," he said, "I still got the honeymoon suite."

I blinked. After a series of shoddy hotel rooms and days spent sitting up in a car, back aching, I was ready for a treat.

"Heart-shaped Jacuzzi," he said.

"Tempting," I said.

"Amway convention," he said, "took up all the rooms in town."

"Wow."

"I'll give you a discount: fifty bucks." I stood before him, trying to decide if renting a honeymoon suite alone was pathetic or empowering, when he added, "Bottle of champagne included."

"Deal," I said.

The room was truly amazing. The heart-shaped tub was just the tiniest bit scummy, and the enormous bed was made up with shiny red sheets. There were faded silk roses strewn willy-nilly around the room, and a dusty copy of *The Joy of Sex* on the night table where the Gideon Bible should have been. It was open, and I wandered over to peer at the line drawing: a ponytailed man entwined with an ample lady, her arms thrown up in ecstasy, hairy armpits exposed. I was startled by a knock at the door.

"Yes?" I called nervously.

"Got your champagne, lady," said the man from the front desk.

I opened the door. He held out a bottle and two glasses. "It's pink champagne," he said. "I'm Al, by the way."

"Oh thanks," I said. "I just need one glass, though."

"Me, too," said Al. He gazed around the room forlornly.

"I'm just here on business," I said, hoping I sounded important.

"Do you like the room?" he asked, and then went on before I could answer, "My wife, she decorated it herself. She was always reading those home and garden magazines."

"It's very nice."

"I told her the roses were too much," he said. He looked up at me. If you ignored the hairdo Al had sculpted out of Brylcreem, he looked sort of sweet. His eyes were watery. "Do you think the roses are too much?" he asked.

"I think they're beautiful," I said.

"She died last year," said Al. "Cancer took her."

I nodded. "My mom, um, just died," I said, but he didn't seem to hear me.

"She was blond until the end," said Al. "You know who she said I looked like?"

"No," I said.

"She said I looked like Elvis. Elvis the Pelvis, she'd call me."

"Al," I said, "would you like some champagne?"

He pulled his cigarettes from his shirt pocket. "Why not?" he said.

We popped the cork, and shared the bottle right there, Al and I. We sat at the faux-marble table, on the velvet chairs. We talked about Al's wife, and my mother. Al said I could call him Elvis if I wanted to.

My plan to find the girl in the photograph was simple. I would start looking in Missoula, where Elvis assured me all the young kids lived, and then I would fan out to Arlee and the surrounding towns.

I made copies of the picture at Bitterroot Copies. With the help of an energetic boy named Stan, I blew up Ellie's laughing face to life size. Step One in *Be Your Own Private Dick* was: "Visit local watering holes, supermarkets, and Laundromats with your photograph. BE AGGRESSIVE!" I got a cup of coffee at Food for Thought and set out with a folder of photocopies. I felt my mother cheering me on.

By four, however, I was exhausted and dispirited. Nobody had seen Ellie, and it seemed that a missing person in Montana was no occasion for excitement. In fact, in a shop window I saw a T-shirt that read: *MONTANA. The last, best place...TO HIDE!* The Laundromat workers and supermarket clerks sighed when I pulled out the grainy picture, and directed me to bulletin boards already filled with faces of lost friends, husbands, children, and dogs. I tacked Ellie's picture up over other, older posters. I wrote my hotel and room number on the bottom of each copy.

I saved the watering holes for last. By nightfall, they were packed with students and drunks. I ordered a Scotch at Al & Vic's, my first stop. The bartender was a genial man named Lew, and the bar was attached to Fran's Hi-Way Café, from which I ordered a fish sandwich. Lew had not seen Ellie.

"Sort of looks like a lot of girls," he noted, lighting a Pall Mall.

I scrutinized the photo. "I guess so," I said.

"Dark hair, nice smile," continued Lew. He added, "They all start out that way." He gestured to a woman who appeared to be asleep in the corner. "She started out that way."

"She still has dark hair," I said.

"True," said Lew. "Haven't seen her smile in some time, though."

"What's her name?" I asked.

"Goes by Lorna."

I nodded. Yet another worn woman, a redhead, brought my fish sandwich to the bar. I showed her Ellie's picture, and she brought it close to her face. "Sort of looks like that stripper," she said.

Good Lord. "What stripper?" I asked, trying to keep my voice even.

"I wouldn't know no stripper," said Lew, looking jumpy.

"She comes in for eggs, some mornings," said the red-haired woman. "Hangs out at Charley B's. And Mulligan's, 'course."

I looked around frantically for a pen. Lew slid a dull pencil over the bar, and I wrote on my napkin, "Charley B's. Mulligan's." The red-haired woman pulled a cigarette from behind her ear and lit it. "She owe you money?"

"No," I said. "Who's Charley B?"

"Dead," said Lew. "Good man, but he had a temper."

"Charley B's is his bar," said the woman. She pointed through the dirty front window. "Right down Higgins," she said.

"Thank you," I said. I ate my sandwich quickly. It was terrible: salty and overcooked.

"Charley B," said Lew, "he liked his rum and Cokes, I'll tell you that."

"Shut up, honey," said the woman, and Lew did.

NINE

Bernard was in a meeting when the phone call came. They were working on the Skidaway subdivision, and Harold was in the middle of his presentation, pointing to a map projected on the wall.

"Sorry, Bernard?" said Jenny, standing in the open doorway, "It's Sarah on the phone. She's at the hospital." Like wildfire, the smiles ignited across the boardroom.

"Don't forget the cigars!" called Jim, as Bernard rushed to his office to gather his things. Take one last look around, he told himself: Things will never be the same.

Sarah told him that her water had broken. They were giving her Pitocin, but there was plenty of time. She'd brought her bag, the crossword puzzles, slippers. Her Yankee voice was sparkling and scared on the phone. "It's happening, Bear," she said. "I can't wait to meet the baby."

"Close your eyes, darlin'," said Bernard. "I'll be there when you open them."

He hit a pothole almost immediately, but he didn't slow

down, veering across three lanes of traffic to make a right on Abercorn. When he finally reached the hospital, the drug had already sent Sarah into a hellish place; she looked up at him wild-eyed and gripped his hand with terrible strength. "Help me," she said. "Help me, goddamn it!"

The hours melted together; he stayed with her every minute, though the nurses pressed him to leave. He slipped ice chips into her mouth, and helped her count through the contractions the way they had learned in the Lamaze class. (It seemed like a different life already, sitting on blankets in that stuffy room, giggling through pretend labor, watching grainy videotapes.)

Sarah told him she couldn't do it, couldn't go on, but she did go on, even when the epidural didn't take. Bernard held her left knee when it was finally time to push, pinning it back to make room for the baby. Sarah's knee was freckled like the rest of her, and the skin turned red underneath his grip. We're having a baby, *he kept telling himself. He had touched Sarah's swelling belly over the months, felt the thudding kicks, had even heard the heartbeat through the doctor's stethoscope. But it hadn't been real. He hadn't believed it, and then there she was.*

Her skull, a perfect arc, and she slid out like water, his daughter. She had toes, fingers! They let Bernard cut the cord, and then they took her away, to clean her up and wrap her in a cheap pink blanket.

"Thank God it's over," said Sarah, her hair tangled, her face swollen.

Bernard gazed at his wife, touched her forehead, but his love was split now. He loved Sarah, but it was a dull and steady love. He yearned for his daughter to come back into the room, missed her fiercely although they just met. Bernard and Sarah decided to name the baby Agnes—it was Sarah's mother's name.

"Darlin'," said Bernard, anticipating his daughter, warm in his arms. "This is just the beginning," he said.

TEN

from the desk of

AGNES FOWLER

Dear Johan,

It was lovely to receive your letter today. The confetti spilling out was certainly a surprise! I didn't know you have confetti in Alaska. Well, truthfully, I never actually thought about whether or not you have confetti in Alaska. I will admit, however, to wondering if you have Bagel Bites. Frances brought Bagel Bites into the library today, and a sweet thought rushed over me, and it was connected to you: I wonder if they have Bagel Bites in Alaska?

I was fascinated by your Personality Plus! Profile. It's a good thing white is your fave color, isn't it? What with all the snow, I mean. In Alaska.

No, I don't think I have read the Hardy Boys books. I didn't read Nancy Drew either. But I do agree that there are mysteries all around us.

Your nightmare about the raven was very scary indeed. I am not trying to be coy by not filling out Number Eight. I guess I'd just like to know you better before I tell you about some things. A girl must have her secrets, don't you think?

On a side note, I am so happy that you enjoy writing letters as much as I do. There is something slow and special about written correspondence. I enjoy composing my notes to you, and I love waiting for a response. It makes my whole day more exciting, wondering what the mailman has in store. So thank you.

In terms of the upcoming AlaskaHunks.com Love Match Cruise, I suppose I could think a bit more about it. I haven't taken too much vacation time, and I don't think I've ever been outside of the Mountain Time Zone. Sometimes I have daydreams about warmer places, maybe my mother told me about them, I don't know.

I'm sorry I didn't put a picture in my first letter. I have what Jon Davies calls "dishwater blond" hair (though I prefer "dirty blond" myself); I'm twenty-one. This picture was taken last year on the fourth of July, at the Arlee Pow-Wow and Rodeo. Arlee is a town right near here. I'm the one with the hamburger. Believe it or not, this picture was in *People Magazine*! There was a special section called "SUMMER FUN." I look like I'm having fun, don't I? I'm not. That was one of my bad days, but enough about that.

So, do you enjoy your work as an Explosives Engineer? I must say, that has a better ring to it than "InterLibrary Loan Clerk." Don't get me wrong–I love my job–but I wish

I got to blow things up. Do you use dynamite? And another question: do people call you up and say, "Johan, we'd like an explosion over here, pronto." Also: did you know when you were a little boy that you wanted to be an Explosives Engineer?

I wanted to be an actress. It's all I talked about when I was little, my father said. I wanted to be famous. But he was against that. He didn't want to share me with anyone, he said. He loved me so much.

One time, we went to Sears, and it happened to be Portrait Day. While my father was buying a garden hose, I watched kids posing against a gray backdrop, smiling for the camera. They tugged at their clothes. I knew not to even ask my father for a portrait. He didn't like television either, or newspapers. He was a strange man, I know that now. Maybe he loved me too much. He used to say I was the light of his life.

Anyway, by the time he died there was no real reason to have my picture taken. Last year, we got Photo IDs for the library, but you wouldn't want my Photo ID, would you? So the magazine picture is all I've got. I hope you will still write me back. I'll be fine if you don't, of course! But I hope you do.

Yrs.,
Agnes Fowler

ELEVEN

Be Your Own Private Dick had advice for approaching the missing person: PLAY IT COOL. After a few days of tacking up my posters and waiting by the phone, I decided to follow one lead I had written on a napkin: Charley B's.

It was awe-inspiringly cold as I walked down Higgins Avenue. I bought a giant down jacket and gloves at the Salvation Army, but even paired with Madeline's snowpants, they did nothing to cut the wind. My face felt as if it were on fire by the time I reached the dim bar called Charley B's. I shoved the door open, and a rush of cigarette smoke and heat bathed my body.

There were pictures of weathered men in frames running along the back wall. Opposite, a long bar stretched out. Most of the ratty barstools were occupied. In the back, a pool table was surrounded by wooden tables. A window cut into the wall advertised the Dinosaur Café. I could see a short-order cook moving behind the window, pulling a basket of fries out of hot oil.

The bar was filled with the hilarity of desperate people around the holidays. Plastic holly was pasted on a mirror, and signs read: PABST PITCHER $5. It looked as if many had gone for the Pabst deal: except for the gaunt fellows drinking whiskey at the bar, everyone was sharing pitchers of beer.

I scanned the crowd as I tacked up the MISSING poster: longhaired students of indeterminate sex in caps and sweaters, grizzled men. There were a few college-age girls who had shed the cocoons of their parkas. I looked over them, but nothing clicked. I took a seat at the bar, among the older drinkers, and ordered a beer.

The woman who slid a cardboard coaster before me was about forty, but wore her frizzy hair in a high ponytail, like a cheerleader. "Two-fifty," she said. Her T-shirt read, "Buy Me a Bud."

"Thanks." I gave her a five.

She returned with my change and a full, cold glass. Her teeth were a mess, but there was something winsome in her smile. "Sure is cold," I said.

"Sorry?"

"It sure is cold, I said. I've never been to Montana before."

"Oh, OK," said the waitress. "Are you going up to Glacier?"

"No," I said, "just staying here." The waitress nodded disinterestedly and turned.

I took a sip of my beer. I had started out my trip so hopefully, feeling as if I were on a mission of some sort. But now

I wasn't sure what to do. I sat at the bar for a while, imagining the lives of the people around me–the boy in the windbreaker, the tattooed girl at his side. What had brought them to a smoky bar in Montana? This felt like a town people came to from somewhere else. In that sense, it reminded me of New Orleans: it was a place you could make into a home if your own home hadn't worked out.

After a few beers, I returned to my honeymoon suite. I tried to call Winnie, but one of her kids told me she was out. Kit was out, too. I sat and stared at the phone, and then I called Madeline. She picked up after one ring. "Hello? Hello?" She sounded panicked.

"Hey," I said, "it's me."

"Oh," she said. "It's late here," she added.

"I'm sorry."

"It's OK," she said. "Hold on while I bring you into the living room." I heard some shuffling, and I imagined Madeline settling on her velvet couch. "I can't sleep anyway," she said. "I'm sick all the time."

"That's awful."

"You got that right. But I guess it's worth it. So, any news?"

"Yes," I said, defensively.

Madeline was silent, and then said, "Well, what?"

I sighed. "I put signs up all over Missoula."

Madeline laughed, meanly. Then she said, "I'm sorry."

"I'm doing the best I can," I said.

"You're living in a dream world," said Madeline.

"Let me, then."

"You called me," said Madeline.

For another week, I schlepped around town in Madeline's snowpants. I tacked up posters and ate greasy food, growing fond of the Hot Pepper Jack Burger at a bar called the Missoula Club. (Locals called it the "Mo Club." I didn't feel like a local yet.)

After one of these burgers and a lonely evening reading *The Joy of Sex,* I woke in the middle of the night. As always, the neon Thunderbird sign shone through my window. I had been dreaming about Ellie walking along Esplanade and reaching my house. She picked pebbles off the ground and threw them at my window. But I couldn't wake up, couldn't walk onto the balcony and look down at her. I was pinned to my bed, and Ellie waited, just outside my line of vision.

I decided to go have a drink. Something must have pulled me out of dreams, because as soon as I walked into Charley B's, I saw her.

TWELVE

from the desk of

AGNES FOWLER

Dear Johan,

Well, OK! It's funny, but right after I sent my last letter, I went for a walk. It's still very cold here in Missoula. (But you know about cold, I suppose.) So I was all bundled up in my new red coat, walking along Higgins Avenue. And what do you know, but I suddenly noticed a sign I've passed one hundred times before. It was a sign in the window of SNAPPY PHOTOGRAPHY STUDIOS, and it said: "Have a sexy portrait taken for that special someone. The perfect gift." And there, underneath the sign, was a photograph of a woman lying on her stomach on a blue divan. Johan, she was nude! My first instinct was to be shocked. I kept walking.

But really, it was cold, so I decided to stop in for a drink at The Bridge. And while I drank my Chardonnay and looked around at all the ruddy students eating pizza, I began to think, well, why not? My father hadn't wanted me to grow up. He adored me, cherished me like a child, but now he was gone, and why shouldn't I have a sexy portrait? I am a woman, now.

It was a few more Chardonnays later, but I went home and called SNAPPY PHOTOGRAPHY STUDIOS. "This is Snappy," said the man who answered.

"Hello," I said, "this is Agnes Fowler."

"Well," said Snappy, "what can I do for you, hon?"

Hon! Nobody had ever called me "hon," as far as I could remember. I have to say I didn't mind.

"Snappy," I said, "I have a special someone, and I'd like a sexy portrait."

"Agnes!" said Snappy, "who's the lucky guy?"

"You don't know him," I said.

"Well, why don't you come in tomorrow at four?" said Snappy. "Bring your favorite dress, and do your hair or whatever."

"I will," I said, and I hung up the phone feeling quite jolly about things. I was up late going through my closet. Needless to say, I didn't have anything to wear for a sexy portrait. I had skirts, blouses, and cardigan sweaters for when it gets chilly in the library. I had two dresses: the one I'd worn to my father's funeral, and the one I'd bought for the Annual Library Picnic and Hoe-Down. The picnic one had big, green lily pads on it. It was nice, as dresses go, but it was not sexy.

I took the day off. In the morning, I headed to the Bon

Marché. The salesgirl was young. Her nametag said Yolanda. (Which sounds like Johan!)

I explained the Sexy Portrait situation to Yolanda, and she got to work. I was embarrassed about my underclothes (I won't go into detail) but Yolanda was on the mark. She brought me a red strapless dress, a black dress that dipped so low in the back it made me blush, an armful of lacy underwear, and a pair of high heels. I bought it all. And then I hit the makeup counter.

Yolanda told the makeup woman to give me the Star Treatment. Oh, I had a lovely time. It was warm, but not too warm, in the Bon Marché. There were soft rock hits playing softly over the PA system. And there aren't any windows or clocks, so I didn't know what time it was as I felt fingers on my face, fingers cool with moisturizer and then foundation. A feathery brush on my cheekbones, a cotton applicator placing eye shadow on my lids. I got mascara and lip-liner and lipstick. Finally, Yolanda held up a mirror.

All I can say is WOW! I looked like a sexpot.

I sashayed over to Olé Hair Salon, doing my best not to get snow on my high heels. A lady shouldn't betray her beauty secrets, Yolanda told me, but I will reveal that you can do wonders with mousse and a hairdryer. I even had time for a glass of wine before my Sexy Portrait appointment.

Snappy almost dropped his Diet Coke when I walked in the door. "Snappy," I said, feeling bold from my makeover and the wine, "how are you, honey?" I leaned in, giving him a good sniff of my J. Lo Glow perfume.

"Agnes," he said, "you look divine."

Snappy put Marvin Gaye on the boom box. He offered me a Diet Coke. He led me into his studio, and there was the blue divan. I sat on it rather stiffly at first, but it wasn't long before Snappy had arranged me in a good lounge, one arm draped above my hair, one resting on my stomach.

Snappy grabbed his camera and got to work. He murmured things like, "Over here, dear" and "That's it!" and "Oh, my, Agnes!" I had a fantastico time on that couch. I changed into both of my new dresses behind a Chinese folding screen, and eventually (you may as well know) Snappy took a few pictures of me in my fancy new lingerie.

Well, OK! So here is the picture you asked for. Maybe I will wear this red dress on the AlaskaHunks.com Love Match Cruise. I still HAVE NOT decided about the cruise, but might approach Frances about it, we'll see. What do you think? How are the stars in June in Alaska?

Sincerely,
Agnes Fowler

THIRTEEN

After the bitter wind outside, the warmth of Charley B's was comforting. The jukebox played, *Sailing takes me away....* I walked to the bar, where Kendra was working. I had finally learned her name, after a few nights spent drinking. I ordered a beer, and took a sip.

And then, across the room, I saw Ellie.

I had to fight for breath. The door to Charley B's swung shut behind me. Ellie wore a tan turtleneck sweater and jeans; her brown hair fell to her shoulders. The line of her nose, her lips, her eyelids were the same. She looked like a child, actually: you could see the young bones underneath her skin. She sat at a table toward the back of the bar with a much older man. The man was tanned. He wore a dirty wool hat.

Ellie–or the girl who looked like Ellie–didn't talk. She looked down into her beer. I wanted to run to her, to touch a part of her, crush her in my arms, but I didn't even take off my coat. I put quarters in the cigarette machine and pulled the lever, a crisp pack of Camels falling into the chute. *Play it cool,* I told myself, *Play it cool.* I walked to the bar.

"Whatcha drinking there?" asked a man sitting on a barstool.

"Uh," I said, "beer." The man was about my age, with a plump face spilling out underneath a baseball cap.

"What *kind* of beer?" he said, smiling. Was this a come-on, I wondered. It would never work in New Orleans.

"Newcastle," I said, turning back toward the table where Ellie was sitting. While I watched, she took one finger and followed the line of her hair, tucking a strand behind her small ear. She picked up her beer and took a sip.

"Faaancy!" said the man next to me.

"Uh," I said.

"How 'bout I buy you a Leinenkugel?" he said, smiling widely.

"I'm fine, thanks."

"Have you ever had a Leinenkugel?"

"Sam," said Kendra, coming forward. "Leave this lady alone, OK?"

"I was just asking," said the man.

"Maybe it's time for you to go on home, Sam," she said.

"OK, OK," said Sam, moving a few stools away from me. "I'll be good, OK."

"Thanks," I said to Kendra.

"It's my job," she said.

"I'm a bartender in New Orleans," I said, wanting the conversation to continue, feeling cold and alone. "Well, cocktail waitress," I clarified.

"Whatever you say, sweetheart," said Kendra, moving away from me. I thought about how many people I had walked away from at The Highball, people trying bravely for some connection. I took a long sip of my beer, and then I faced Sam.

"Maybe I would like that Leinenkugel," I said.

"All right!" said Sam.

I looked around, then, and Ellie was standing, pulling on her coat, her beer half-finished. I stubbed out my cigarette. The man took Ellie by the upper arm, gripping tight, and led her to the back exit.

"Never mind," I said. "I've got to go." I grabbed my parka and hat.

"Hold on," said Sam. "You just got here."

"Sorry," I said, and rushed toward the exit. I pushed past groups of people and reached the heavy door, opening it and running outside. But I was too late. The snowy street was empty.

The next morning, I bought the *Missoulian* newspaper and a bagel with strawberry cream cheese and sat on my motel bed. Now it was just a matter of waiting, I knew. Ellie was in Missoula, and Missoula was a small town. Eventually I would run into her again. I just needed to bide my time.

I flipped through the Real Estate section, the Want Ads. And there it was:

Pianist needed. Apply in person. Cee Cee's Cocktails, 30 North Front Street.

I was a pianist, wasn't I? I held out my fingers in front of me. I needed a manicure. But otherwise, they were in working order. I opened the bedside drawer and found a phone book, flipped to the "Salon" listings. I called and made a manicure appointment at Nail Me, Baby.

Cee Cee was a heavyset woman with short hair. Her previous pianist was a blind man named Karl. "He moved to Texas," she said, shaking her head at his folly. Cee Cee's was a tough-looking establishment: faded gold wallpaper, dim lights. It was once a brothel, Cee Cee told me wistfully.

She showed me to a ratty baby grand. "Make me cry," she said. She lit a cigarette, put one hand on her hip. I rested on the stool. Two early drinkers watched me.

I hadn't played seriously in years. I closed my eyes and tried to think about Cee Cee. She did not look like an unhappy woman, but everyone had some unhappiness in them. How would I touch on that spot, then ease it with soaring notes? I began to play "Through with Love," first tentatively, then with gusto. It felt good to perform, and my fingers seemed to move on their own. I finished, and Cee Cee said, "You sing?"

"Um," I said.

"Great," she said. "You can start Monday. But get some clothes, sweetie. A long dress. A gown." She squinted. "You got a gown?"

"Um," I said.

"Great," she said, "Monday at six."

I tried to think of what to say, but Cee Cee began to cough–a hacking, smoker's cough–and so I nodded instead and left.

*

That weekend, still looking for things to occupy my time, I read about the Lolo Dog Sled Races in the *Missoulian.* I decided to head over. Early on Saturday morning, I boarded the shuttle outside the Thunderbird. There were a few other people on the bus: a girl with greasy hair writing furiously in a reporter's notebook, a loudmouth man telling whoever would listen about the upcoming ice climbing festival. (He was a sponsor, it seemed.) The bus wound its way out of Missoula, heading into the Idaho mountains. Lolo was a cross-country ski and ski-mobile area, but this weekend it was all about dogs.

When the shuttle bus stopped, I stepped off. It was snowing and windy: flakes whipped sideways against my face. I shaded my eyes and saw ten or so trucks parked alongside each other. Each truck was surrounded by all sorts of dogs: fluffy ones, curly-tailed ones, ones that looked like wolves, even some hounds. The first truck I reached was red, with Wyoming license plates. The bed held a kennel for the dogs; they ate from bowls of food and water. As I approached, the dogs ran to me, pulling against their chains. One leapt up and his paws hit my chest. I laughed out loud.

"They like attention," said a voice. I looked up: it was the man who had been sitting with Ellie at Charley B's. The one with the dirty wool hat. His eyes were very pale blue: the color of ice. Graying hair curled from underneath his hat. He was sexy, but also hard. He scared me.

"Are these your dogs?" I asked.

"No," he said. "I just train and run them. The owner's in

Jackson Hole."

"They're beautiful," I said.

The man held out his hand. His fingernails were dirty. "I'm Daven," he said.

"Caroline," I said. His grip was strong.

"That one's Jetta. He's an Alaskan Husky," said Daven, pointing to the dog with its paws on my chest.

"Jetta?"

"The owner names them after cars," said Daven. I petted the dog. "I'm racing the six-dog in an hour," he said. Another dog jumped up on me, El Camino. "You want to help?" said Daven.

"What?"

"I need one more person to hold them back. You just grab onto Forester, she's the lead dog. You hold her collar until it's time for us to go."

"I'd love to," I said. I was flustered, and couldn't tell if he was flirting with me.

"Great," said Daven, "I appreciate it."

I bought a cup of coffee under a tent and drank it in the warming hut, a tepee with hay on the floor and a propane heater. Two old ladies came in and discussed a woman named Shirley. After my coffee, I went back to Daven's red truck. The racing area was filling up with people. I could see the starting line, where speakers had been set up. The Rolling Stones blared through the snow: "Brown Sugar." I realized that I was grinning from ear to ear.

Jetta jumped on me again as soon as I approached the truck. "Hi, Jetta," I said. "Hi, Jetta." She breathed, hot, into my face.

"Hey, there," said Daven, opening the driver's-side door and stepping from his truck, "this is Charlene."

She climbed out of the truck slowly, a brown boot and a slim expanse of denim. A pink pom-pom hat and then the swinging hair. She lifted her head and I gasped. It was Ellie.

She smiled in greeting. Her teeth were perfectly aligned, but discolored. She was so young—what was she doing with this man? She looked unhealthy, too skinny. My heart broke.

"Hi," I said.

"Hi!" she said, holding out her hand. I took it, touching her skin.

"I'm Caroline," I said, looking straight at her, willing her to know me.

She did not meet my gaze. Her eyes were lit with a creepy fervor, and they darted around unnervingly. Her pupils were dilated. She was on some drug, I could tell. "Caroline's going to help you hold them back," said Daven. I nodded.

"Great," said Ellie, still looking away from me. "That's so great. Babe, can I have a smoke?" The way she spoke was rapid and breathy.

"Just one," said Daven, fishing a pack from his pocket. Ellie's hand shook as she reached for the cigarette. "You want one, Caroline?" he asked.

"Sure." We stood and smoked. This was the moment I had driven across the country for, but now that it had arrived, I felt paralyzed. It hadn't occurred to me that Ellie wouldn't recognize me, or that Ellie would be called Charlene.

The snow fell hard, and the dogs strained at their chains. My feet were beginning to get cold, but I didn't want to leave Ellie for another second. I kept thinking of things to say to jar her memory: *I'm visiting from New Orleans*, or *My sister Madeline loves dogs, too....* But nobody was talking.

"Are you from Montana?" asked Daven.

"No," I said. "Actually, I'm just visiting. From New Orleans."

"The Big Easy," said Daven.

"Wow," said Ellie, "New Orleans. Wow. New Orleans." Her fast speech was making me nervous.

"Have you ever been there?" I asked.

"No, no I don't think so," said Ellie. She ran her tongue over her lips. They were very dry. As I looked at her closely, I saw that she had a thin sheen of sweat on her face.

"Are you...," I began. "Are you from around here?" I said.

Daven looked at Ellie, a sharp look. I saw it. "No," said Ellie, too loud.

"Nobody's from here. We're all from somewhere else, right?" said Daven.

"I don't know," I said.

"You looking for some work?" said Daven.

"What?" I said. "No."

"Do you have a job already?" said Ellie.

"Actually—" I said, but Daven cut me off, motioning to his watch.

"Time for the race," he said.

He and Ellie untangled six harnesses and strapped the

dogs to the wooden sled. Daven stood on the back of the sled and steered the dogs by putting pressure on the skis. There was a big brake, just in case. We held fast to the dogs' collars and made our way to the starting line.

There were dozens of people now, and dogs yelped and sang, pulling at their harnesses. The music blared (Aerosmith: "Love in an Elevator"), and the emcee announced the start of the race. It was a six-mile course through the woods: a large map of the trail was posted. Daven's team was third, and we watched the other teams start.

"We are ready!" yowled the emcee, announcing the first team. "Lining up right here. It's Craig Land, of Whitefish, Montana. His lead dog is Pee-Wee. Are you ready, handlers? In ten, nine, eight, seven...." The dogs made noises I had never heard before, snarling and pulling at their harnesses, leaping into the air with excitement. The sight of the groomed racetrack drove the dogs wild. When the countdown ended, Craig Land—a tall man in a fur hat—jumped into his sled and the handlers let go. The dogs shot forward, pulling the sled, and Craig Land, behind them.

The next team was led by a woman. Daven told me that the woman, Vivian Mason, used the dogs to get to and from her house in the winter. She lived off the grid, outside Bonner. Her dogs were Alaskan huskies. At the end of the countdown, her handlers let go, and Vivian was off like a shot. It was Daven's turn.

Ellie and I held the two lead dogs. I had Forester, a big husky with one brown eye and one blue. He was impatient, and almost pulled me onto the ground. But I held fast, and the countdown began. Daven pulled his dirty hat on tight, and finally it was time. I let go, and Forester ran. Daven leaned back, bent his knees, and was gone.

I put my fingers on Ellie's arm. "Want some hot chocolate?" I asked. She looked noncommittal. We went back to the blue tent, and then the warming hut. Now that we were finally together, I couldn't find a word to say. She seemed very tense.

"So," I said, "how'd you meet Daven?"

"On the Internet."

Good Lord, I thought.

"Do you like Montana?" I asked.

"I guess so," she said. "It's fine."

"You don't look like a Charlene," I said.

Ellie's eyes snapped open. She looked alarmed, but tried to cover up. "Well, I don't know who does," she said. "Look like their name, I mean."

"Is that your real name?" I asked.

"Of course!" said Ellie, unconvincingly. "Let's go outside."

"OK," I said. We made our way to the finish line. We stood in the snow, and Ellie whispered something to me.

"What?" I said.

"You look like a Caroline," said my sister, and we watched the dog teams in the distance, racing toward the finish.

As time went on, she seemed to calm down. When the race was over, we waited by the truck while Daven fed the dogs. "So I'm playing piano at Cee Cee's Cocktails. You should come hear me sometime," I said.

Ellie pushed a strand of hair behind her ear. "You never know," she said.

"How long until Daven will be done?"

"He'll be here all day."

She kept talking, telling me about Daven and his dogs, about how much they both loved animals. "I put a picture of a lynx cub on our wall at the Wilma," she said.

"The Wilma?"

"It's the tall building on the river. That's where we live."

I knew the place she was talking about: it was the only skyscraper in Missoula, a tall stone building with a marquee in front. "I thought that was a movie theater."

"It is, downstairs," she said.

"Is the rent cheap?" I asked.

"Cheapest in town. You looking?"

"Maybe," I said.

"I could introduce you to the landlady later."

Finally, something was happening, even if it was leading to a lease on a crappy apartment. "Sounds great," I said.

"You got a job?" asked the withered woman in the basement offices of the Wilma.

"Yes, ma'am," I said.

"Call me Diane," she said, taking a drag of her Virginia Slim. "What's your job?"

"I'm a piano player at Cee Cee's Cocktails," I said.

"Cee Cee," said Diane, practically spitting the name.

"It's on Front Street...."

Diane stubbed out her cigarette. "I know where Cee

Cee's is," she said. Ellie and I followed her into an old elevator lined in striped wallpaper. Diane closed the elevator door with a shove and sank onto a stool in the corner of the elevator: a furry stool with gold tassels.

"Is Caroline going to be on my floor?" said Ellie, giddily. She seemed excited to be friends with me.

"Same bathroom even," said Diane. "Same phone."

"Excuse me?" I said.

Ellie leaned toward me. "We have a shared bathroom on the second floor," she said. "It's not bad, really. There are only two of us. Well, three now!" She smiled. "And there's a pay phone in the hallway," she added.

On the second floor, Diane heaved herself to her feet and opened the elevator. "Home sweet home," she rasped.

The hallway was carpeted in an orange plush. Two framed pictures hung crookedly: a monkey clinging to a branch, and a litter of kittens in a basket. I smelled tomato sauce. "This is the bathroom," said Diane, opening a door into a small but tidy room with a shower, toilet, and sink.

"That's my potpourri," said Ellie, "and my little starfish soaps." My head was reeling; Ellie had collected starfish on the beach when we were small.

"Apartment 204," said Diane, opening a door directly across the hall from the bathroom. I made my way inside. The apartment was already filled with brown furniture. It was made up of three rooms: a living room, a tiny kitchen with a weird latticework wall, and a bedroom with a sink in it. "Used to be a dentist's office," noted Diane.

"Oh," I said.

"Look at the view," said Ellie.

The view was stunning. Although my windows were on either side of the marquee, I could see the mountains and the Clark Fork River.

"It's a month-to-month lease, right?" I said.

"Sure, honey," said Diane.

"You are going to love it here," said Ellie, clapping her hands together. Her actions felt false to me, contrived. But I just went with the moment. I didn't have anything to go home to, really, and maybe this girl was my sister after all. I tried to ignore the uneasy feeling in my stomach. Maybe, as my mother had told me, I was just afraid of being happy.

"I'll take it," I said.

That night, after I moved my things into the Wilma, Ellie and I bought a bottle of wine and a big sandwich to split from the market down the street. I paid. We sat in my bedroom, watching the moon over the mountains. Ellie drank the wine, but barely ate any of the sandwich. "I'm so tired," she said, "but I've got to work later."

"Eat something," I said.

"I'm just not so hungry," she said.

"So what brought you to Montana?"

She sipped her wine. "Daven," she said, simply.

We sat in silence. I was breathless, wondering if Ellie was going to touch me, curl up with her head in my lap as she had so long ago. "What's your real name?" I said.

She looked at me. Her eyes were dull now. "I can't–" said Ellie.

"Yes you can," I said. I put my hand on her knee.

She stood. "I'm really tired," she said.

I held my breath, but I knew I had to give her time. "Sure," I said. Ellie stood up and hugged me. Her body felt unfamiliar, but warm.

It was only when I brought my deposit check to Diane that I found out Ellie made a hundred bucks as soon as I signed on the dotted line.

PART THREE

ONE

THE DAY BERNARD'S DAUGHTER DROWNED was bright and cloudless. Five-year-old Agnes awoke early, running into Bernard and Sarah's bedroom and yelling, "Beach! Beach!" Sarah sighed and rolled over, and Bernard climbed from bed and pulled on his bathrobe.

"After coffee," he told her.

Bernard and Agnes sat in the kitchen of the Tybee cottage, planning the day. They would go to the Breakfast Club for waffles, and then fish before lunch at the Crab Shack Restaurant. Little Agnes loved the Crab Shack, which had holes in the center of the tables for throwing shrimp shells. After lunch, they would head to the beach until dinnertime.

Sarah was still in bed. "Momma!" said Agnes, standing at the foot of the bed with her hands on her hips.

"Oh for the love of Christ," said Sarah. Bernard winced. Her brash language had lost its charm for him.

"Why don't you meet us there?" he said.

"Order me a waffle, will you?" said Sarah, and then she

rolled into her pillow.

Bernard and Agnes walked along the beach to the Breakfast Club. Bernard's family cottage was the second one built on Tybee Island; condominiums and motels surrounded it now.

At the diner, there was a wait, so Bernard and Agnes took stools at the counter. "Who do you think is the happiest man in this room?" asked Bernard. He watched Agnes as she looked around, taking in the ruddy-faced fishermen, the college students on break. "Him," she said finally, pointing with her little finger at the fry cook named Will, who winked at her and wiped his forehead with the back of his hand. Will had a ponytail, a Harley tattoo, and a soft spot for Agnes.

"Wrong, darlin'," said Bernard, touching her curls with his palm. "It's me."

"You're weird, Daddy," said Agnes, sipping her orange juice.

Sarah arrived, disheveled and begging for coffee. After breakfast, they stopped at Chu's for bait, and then walked down Tybrisa Street to the beach. The fishing pier was deserted, save for one young boy with a large fishing rod. Sarah unfolded her chair on the sand. Agnes stayed with her father, and he helped her bait her hook.

"I'm cold," said Sarah, after about an hour. She had left her chair and walked out to the end of the pier. Her feet were bare. "And," she said, "this book is dull." She held up the book, a history of Tybee. Her nose was pink, and freckles stood out on her cheeks. She wore an old cardigan around her shoulders.

"One more cast?" said Bernard. He was getting chilly, too, and nothing was biting. The water was dark underneath the

pier, and the boy had left.

"I'm not cold," said Agnes.

"Not long until the Crab Shack, A," said Sarah, swatting Agnes on her behind. Agnes wore flip-flops, a plastic visor, and a green terrycloth sweatshirt over her bathing suit.

"I'm not cold," Agnes said again. She brought her rod back and cast, a perfect sweep into the water. Bernard looked up and saw clouds swelling. He wished he could walk over to Doc's Bar and have a pint of beer with Sarah. They could wait out the storm and then go back to the big house and make love, the way they had before Agnes.

"We've got to go, baby," he said.

"I don't want to," said Agnes.

Irritation shot through him. "Suit yourself," said Sarah. "Come on, Bear."

"OK," said Bernard. He began to pack up his bait. "Don't want to be without you," he said to Agnes, but he left, walking slowly back to the beach along the pier.

When he looked back, she was smiling, running after him.

On the beach that afternoon, Agnes built sand castles while Sarah and Bernard dozed. There was a man flying an enormous kite by the rocks. He needed both hands to control the red and blue expanse of fabric. "It's like an extra cloud," said Agnes, shading her eyes and looking up at the kite.

"Don't go near the rocks, love," said Sarah, her eyes closed. They had drunk wine with lunch, and they were drowsy.

"I'm not," said Agnes. The wet sand coated her legs, and the wind whipped her hair. The sun broke through the clouds.

When Bernard opened his eyes, Agnes was no longer sitting in front of him. There was an imprint of her in the sand, and her castle was tall and lumpy. Bernard stood quickly and called her name.

Sarah sat up like a shot. "Where is she?" she said, but Bernard was running toward the rocks. "How long was I asleep?" said Sarah. "How long was I asleep?" she repeated.

The man with the kite was on the other side of the rocks now. Bernard yelled for Agnes, and the man came over. "She was right there," he said, "I saw her." He pointed to the edge of the rocks. Waves smashed against the place. Agnes was nowhere, but Bernard discovered one flip-flop tangled in seaweed.

They found her body later that day. She had slipped and hit her head, falling into the water. Sarah clawed at the police officer who came to tell them. She screamed, "It's not true! It's not true!" but Bernard knew it was true.

TWO

I DID NOT SEE ELLIE for over a week. I heard her stepping off the elevator, late at night. The walls in the building were thick, but sometimes I heard Daven's voice. He sounded angry, which made me nervous.

I went to Albertson's Supermarket. The line was long, and I had a while to think. I thought about the day my parents brought Ellie home from the hospital. She was born in February, and had been wrapped in blankets to protect her from the winter wind.

Madeline and I stood in the hallway of our house, waiting for her. We heard the car pull up, and the laughter of our parents. They had been happy once. The front door opened, and icy air hit my face. They bustled in, my parents and my new sister. My father took my mother's coat.

I remember looking at Ellie for the first time. She was ugly, and her hair was dark. My mother bent down and said, "Caroline, it's your sister, Ellie." I reached toward her, and Ellie grabbed my finger. Her grip was tight. Her eyes were big and blue. She blinked like a fish. She held on as if she'd never let go, but then she did.

THREE

from the desk of

AGNES FOWLER

Dear Johan,

There is a masturbator in the library! It shouldn't be so exciting, but we're in that end-of-winter time where everyone is just looking for something to happen. You would think by now that it would be warm. Well, maybe YOU wouldn't.

By the way, I very much enjoyed your last letter. I am flattered that all the Explosives Engineers liked my portrait, but maybe you could keep it to yourself from now on? Just a thought. Also, your poem, "The Stars in June," was divine. And you found so many words to rhyme with "June." I never would have thought of "saloon." But then, I'm not a poet, like you.

It was a graduate student who discovered the masturbator. The student was on the third floor, looking for a book on the Aboriginal tribes of Western Australia. (These people have been persecuted for generations, she informed me.) And right there, in the 994.004s, was a man pleasuring himself! The graduate student, Wendy Weekham, was very upset. She ran downstairs to the Reference Desk and told the student worker the whole story.

Well! A team (made up quickly of student workers and Deanna, the Science Librarian) went right to the third floor, but the masturbator was nowhere to be found. The library went into lockdown. It was just like a movie: we had to eat those tuna sandwiches from the vending machine for lunch, and the police came and looked at every square inch of the library. The masturbator had escaped.

Well, what with all the excitement, I did not get a chance to speak with Frances about the Love Match Cruise. I know the deadline is very soon, so I will try to have some news in my next letter.

Johan, I would like you to know something about me. There is something wrong with my brain. I don't know how else to say it. I'm not stupid, it's the opposite, actually. I think too much, that's what my father always said. Maybe I'll just answer Number Eight, and you can see what you think and if you still want to meet me in person.

8. Worst Nightmare

Ever since I can remember, I have the same dream/nightmare:

I am asleep, and there are two other people sleeping next to me. They smell like applesauce. I'm in a room, somewhere warm. It's raining outside.

When I have this vision, I ache for these two other people, though I am not sure who they are. They look like me—they are my sisters. But my father insisted I did not have any sisters. I am an only child, and yet I can hear the breathing of these two people. I can close my eyes and feel them, beside me. I want to open my eyes, and see who is next to me, but I am too afraid. I lie there, in the night.

Sometimes, I will be in my own living room, reading one of my books (my name is right there, written on the inside flap: Property of Agnes Fowler), and a slow knowledge comes over me. I do not belong where I am, and I am not Agnes Fowler. I am someone else, and there is a different life waiting for me to return.

Johan, what do you make of all this?

Sincerely Yours,
Agnes

P.S. Here is another Sexy Portrait, but please do not share it among the other Explosives Engineers.

FOUR

FROM THE PAY PHONE in the hallway, I called Winnie. "So I got an apartment," I said.

"In Montana? What are you, insane?" Winnie's voice made me smile.

"Have you found a job?" I asked.

"Peggy's gonna be a model," said Winnie.

"No!"

"Yes. She got herself an agent and all that. And Kit's got me working at the auto shop, but I hate it."

"I got a job," I said.

"Girl, doing what?"

"Playing the piano."

"Excuse me?"

"Playing the piano. At a nightclub," I said.

"Are you going to stay there, in Montana? You've already got a life, Caroline, don't forget it."

"I know."

"And what about your long-lost sister?"

The phone was near Ellie's door, so I whispered, "I've met someone, and she looks like she could be Ellie, but I guess I don't know."

"What were you expecting?"

"Something else."

Winnie was silent for a while, and then she said, "Well, come on home. Kit says 'hey.'"

"Tell him I said 'hey.'"

Around four every afternoon, I went to Cee Cee's. I warmed up, ate dinner, and played until eleven or so. The crowd was genial and shabby. One night, I started in with "Scenes from an Italian Restaurant." Billy Joel always got them going. Cee Cee had supplied me with sheet music for all the cocktail standards. She liked Sinatra best, so I tried to throw in "The Lady Is a Tramp" for her. When I played it that night, Cee Cee came right over and dropped a twenty in my tip jar. I gave her "These Boots Were Made for Walking," just for good measure.

At the end of the night, I was feeling good and drunk from the free drinks Cee Cee brought me as I played. I walked home through the lit streets, over the bridge. I looked down at the slow-moving river, imagining the fish that lived in its waters. It was bitter cold, so different from New Orleans. I missed my little apartment and my cat.

I reached the Wilma and rang for the elevator. It arrived, with Diane inside. "How's Cee Cee?" she asked, as she struggled to close the elevator door.

"Fine," I said.

Diane shook her head. "I'll just *bet* she is," she said. We reached the second floor, and I helped Diane open the door. "Good night, now," she said.

"Good night."

It was too late to call Madeline, but I did it anyway. "Where have you *been*?" she said, answering on the fourth ring.

"What do you mean?"

"Every time I call, someone picks up the phone but doesn't say anything," said Madeline. "What the hell is going on?"

"It wasn't me," I said. "The phone's in the hallway, so it must have been someone else."

"The hallway? Jesus," said Madeline.

Around me, the shadowy building was silent, and I was alone. "I think I found her," I whispered.

"What?" said Madeline. "I can't hear you."

"Nothing."

"Talk to me!" said Madeline. "Come home."

I don't even know where that is, I almost said. Instead, I said, "Not now."

It was very dark outside when I heard Ellie leaving her apartment. I was tired of sitting around: I decided to follow her. The elevator arrived, and when I heard her step on it, I slipped into my coat and snowpants. By taking the back stairway, I reached the street in time to see Ellie walking quickly, a block away from me.

It was freezing cold, and I jammed my hands into my

pockets. Madeline's pants made a swishing sound. I saw Ellie's red coat through snowflakes. The street was slippery under my cheap boots.

I crossed Higgins and hung back as she entered a doorway. I ran across the street, almost getting run over by a brown VW van, and followed her into The Oxford, a well-lit diner. It was nearly midnight. A linoleum counter faced a board with the specials spelled out in plastic letters: CHICKEN FRIED STEAK, TEXAS TOAST, BRAINS & EGGS. The men at the counter drank beer with their food. Ellie was nowhere to be seen.

From the corner of the diner, a cheap melody rang out from a Keno machine. Next to the Keno machine was a red curtain. I walked toward the back, checking in the dingy ladies' room, and then stopping by the red curtain. From behind it, I heard, *Pour some sugar on me....* I took a breath—no one seemed to be watching me—and pulled the curtain back.

There was a room beyond the curtain. A club, to be exact. A fat man on a stool looked me up and down. "Five dollars," he said. I opened my wallet, and pulled out a ten. He handed me five wrinkled ones as change. "Have fun," he said with a creepy grin.

I walked into the club (it was Mulligan's, the other name on my napkin, I found out later) and the music pounded against my head. Def Leppard gave way to Whitesnake. I went to the bar and ordered a Jack and Coke. From the bar, I could see the stage, where a desperately skinny woman shook her body back and forth. She was completely nude, trying her best to keep the beat in her drugged-out state. Some man in a cowboy hat held up a bill, and she moseyed over to him, turned completely around, and bent forward. He stuck the bill between her butt cheeks. It was a one-dollar bill. I looked down into my drink, feeling sick and sad.

The girl skipped around. Her hair was limp, her eyes glassy. There were about twenty people in Mulligan's. I was the only woman, and I did not see Ellie. The music thumped on.

Finally, the drugged-out girl limped offstage. The music stopped. After a few minutes, people began grumbling. I ordered another drink, just whiskey this time. I had a bad feeling about what was going to happen, and I was right.

The trippy sounds of Moby wound into the club, and she slinked onstage in a red shortie nightgown and robe. High-heeled patent-leather boots. The midnight showstopper: Ellie.

She had always loved to dance. I thought of her ballet lessons, her chubby frame in pale leotards, recitals on the high school stage. Even taking a walk through our neighborhood, Ellie danced ahead of us, moving her arms to a rhythm the rest of us couldn't hear. She'd pull Madeline or me to our feet, begging us to tango with her. It hit me, as I sat in the seedy Montana strip club: what I had missed. Visions of Ellie swam before me. Ellie at sixteen, at twenty. What Ellies had existed between the hopeful girl I had known and the rough woman gyrating before me now?

There was nothing familiar in Ellie's movements. Her body seemed liquid, and her eyes were half closed. Her head lolled on her neck as if it wasn't quite attached. She was in another world. As I watched, she unzipped one boot, and then the other. The men by the stage were hooting, but I couldn't see anything sexy about her. Her breasts were large, much larger than mine or Madeline's. Perhaps she had had them done. I imagined her in some doctor's office, her upper arm encircled by a man's large hand. She raised her arms above her head–a cheerless imitation of the ballet she had learned as a child–and she stepped from her boots.

Barefoot, she whirled around the stage. The music switched to Portishead–low, slow notes. The bar seemed entranced. Ellie slipped her robe from her shoulders and let it fall down her arms. It was cheap polyester, but Ellie made it look like the finest silk as it slid over her skin. She caught it between two fingers and it trailed from her, rippling in the smoky air. The room was very hot: protection against the brittle chill outside. This whole place was about fortification, I realized, something to get you through the bare, cold nights. New Orleans had plenty of strip clubs, don't get me wrong, but the sheer desperation in Mulligan's made me scared. Men watched Ellie as if they wanted to devour her. They watched with agony, with anger.

Ellie let go of the robe. She was barefoot now, in the red nightie. She brought her arms up again, and again I saw her at four, standing onstage in a pink tutu, a sequined tiara in her hair.

"Take it off, Charlene!" yelled a bearded man.

"Yeah, girl!" chimed in another voice.

She did not appear to hear them. She spun slowly, then with greater speed. She spun until it was hard to see any specific part of her. Her hair melted into her jawbone, the red dress leapt into flame, her ankles were nothing more than a blur. Finally, she stopped. Her face was flushed, and a few strands were stuck to her cheek. Her eyes were closed, and she slowly let one arm fall forward, her white palm opening, as if waiting for someone's hand to slip inside. She was still, her ribcage rising and falling. The song ended, and she stood in silence.

"Charlene!" yelled the bushy man. "Come on, honey."

The music had ended, and the faint ping of the Keno machine was the only accompaniment. She reached to her shoulder and untied the ribbon that held up the nightgown. No one lifted a drink, or made a sound. Ellie touched the other shoulder. She pulled the ribbon, and the nightgown fell.

I could not turn away. Ellie's body was revealed; small-boned, the color of milk. Her stomach was soft. She had shaved her pubic hair, which made her look disturbingly childlike. She opened her eyes, came out of whatever dream had held her. She paused, blinking, naked. Her look was blank, faintly confused. After a few seconds, she bent, collected her clothes, and walked off the stage.

ZZ Top came blaring over the speakers, and another girl took the spotlight, a feisty brunette with a feather boa. I had seen enough.

I drew the red curtain aside, and the halogen lights of the diner made me wince. I zipped my ridiculous parka and pulled my hat over my ears. Cold smacked me in the face when I opened the door, pushing tears from my eyes and burning my lungs.

The sky was empty. I felt raw inside. I suddenly wanted to play piano, to let my sadness flow from my fingertips. A melancholy tune began to well up in my chest.

It had been years since I had heard music playing in my body. Throughout my childhood, I had been trotted out to play for guests, zipped into velvet dresses for my twice-yearly recitals. But when Ellie disappeared, the shining notes went with her. There had been a time when I had fallen asleep listening to my own music. Though I labored through my music major at University of New Orleans, playing steady, uninspired sonatas, dutifully practicing, the joy of composing fled me little by little, and I was left with only technical talent. I could play whatever you put in front of me. If I sat at the piano without sheet music, however, my fingers were clumsy. After college, I stopped playing entirely.

But in the middle of the street, the Oxford Diner sign on one side of me and the mountains on the other, I felt the saddest song fill me. I stood under the fading stars, trying to convince myself that the tears frozen in my eyelashes were from the wind.

FIVE

SARAH HAD BEEN GONE for a long time before she finally packed her things and left Bernard. She didn't write a note, or say goodbye. It didn't matter by then. Like his wife told him, Bernard died when five-year-old Agnes sank into the waves. He had not gone near the ocean since, fishing only in the river, where it was safe.

He was a walking cadaver, Sarah said accusingly, and wasn't worth a damn to anyone. It was, she said, as if he didn't even want to get better. He held onto his grief, spent every night alone in the attic reading fishing catalogs and tying flies. He didn't have anything left for her...couldn't even say her name, could he? Go on, dammit, say my name! Say it! Sarah!

He couldn't say it.

Bernard stood at the upstairs window and watched Sarah pack the car. She took the lamp they had brought home from Bermuda, and the telephone table that had been her grandmother's. She went in and out of the house, fitting into the car the objects she imagined a new life around, and Bernard felt nothing.

Sarah came out carrying something in her arms: the bedspread. She had made it when Agnes was an infant, stitching his old T-shirts next to scraps of her own dresses and shirts. She'd fitted in a square of Agnes' baby blanket and a sliver of Bernard's flannel pajamas when they fell to shreds. Bernard watched Sarah place the blanket carefully in the backseat. The afternoon light filtered through the stained-glass window, casting colored shapes onto his bare feet. It was probably a weekday, and he should probably go to work.

SIX

I BEGAN THE NIGHT with a Cole Porter medley. It was a Friday, and Ccc Ccc's had a bigger crowd than usual: a mixture of drunks and divorcées out on the town. One spiffed-up couple twirled around the floor, showing off their Lindy lessons. My fingers flew over the keys, and my singing voice got better as the night went on.

At some point, I looked toward a dim corner and saw Ellie and Daven watching me. Daven held her hand on the tabletop.

After "Let's Do It (Let's Fall in Love)," I took a break. My tip jar was jammed with small bills. I went into the restroom. When I stepped out of my stall, there was Ellie, leaning against the mirror. "Hi," she said.

"Hi."

"Caroline?"

"Yes?"

"Can I talk to you about something?" she said, putting her hand on my arm. I could see her behind me in the mirror: we had the same eyes, same mouth. I remembered eating blueberry pancakes with Ellie at the kitchen table, the way she would lick the syrup off her lips.

I pulled my lipstick from my purse. In the mirror, I looked drunk. However, my hair looked good, all piled on my head and curled with the curling iron I had found at the Salvation Army. "OK," I said.

"Um, I'm a little short on rent this month."

I swallowed hard. "Yeah?" I said.

"I was just wondering," said Ellie, "if I could borrow, like a hundred dollars? I'll pay you back. I promise."

"Don't you make enough at Mulligan's?" I asked.

"Well," she said, looking down. "Not this month." She was a bad liar. "You're a beautiful piano player, Caroline. Daven really liked it, too."

"Thanks, El," I said.

Her eyes narrowed. "What did you call me?"

"Nothing," I said.

"Oh," she said.

"Let me get my purse," I said.

Back in the apartment building, I was brushing my teeth when someone tried to turn the knob on the bathroom door.

"Um, one minute," I said.

"Sorry," called a voice. It was Ellie. I rinsed my mouth out and opened the door, but no one was in the hallway. I clenched my fists, and went to Ellie's apartment. I knocked.

"Who is it?"

"Charlene? It's me, Caroline."

She opened the door a crack. I could see only her feverish eyes. “What?” she said. “What is it?”

“Let me in,” I said.

“No.” She shut the door firmly. I stood in the hallway for a minute, frustrated and confused. “It’s me,” I said finally. “It’s Caroline.” There was no answer.

In all my dreams of Ellie, I never imagined she might turn into someone I didn’t want to know. It didn’t occur to me that having her in my life could make it worse. I imagined a grown-up version of the baby sister I had known. I didn’t dream past the soft lips on my cheek, the head in my lap, the silky feel of her skin, the cocktails we would share on my New Orleans balcony.

SEVEN

A FEW NIGHTS LATER, I heard Daven yelling at Ellie. I couldn't hear the words, just the anger. It was excruciating. She needed me, and I didn't know how to help her. I envisioned Ellie falling into my arms. She would tell me how much she had yearned for me–how she, too, had felt as if she were missing a part of herself. I wondered what it would feel like to know where she had been for so many years.

Finally, I heard Daven stomp down the hallway and into the elevator. When I was sure he was gone, I went to her room. I banged on the door. "Let me in," I said, with more strength than I felt.

"Leave me alone," said Ellie.

"It's me," I said. "Ellie, it's me!"

The door opened slowly. I could see the mountains beyond her windows, silhouetted against the sky. She stood in a bathrobe. Her face was sunken in around the bones. "What?" she said, and then she began to cry and lurched toward me.

I pulled her in. "Ellie," I said, into her dirty hair. "It's OK, little one. I'm here."

Her body relaxed. She smelled sour, and she sobbed into my shoulder. "I don't know what to do," she said.

Here it was at last: the moment I had waited for. We could live together in New Orleans, as I had promised so long ago. "Come home, El," I said.

When she pulled away, her eyes were pleading. "Why are you calling me that?" she said. "Stop calling me that," she said.

"I'm sorry," I said. "But don't you know who I am?" She looked down. The roots of her hair were light.

"I just need a drink," she said. Her head snapped back. "Let's go get a drink."

"OK," I said.

I had a bad feeling in my stomach as I brushed my hair and put my wallet in my bag. I met Ellie by the elevator. She still looked terrible, but had pulled on a tiny denim miniskirt and her red coat. Her legs were bare.

"You're going to freeze," I said.

"Whatever," said Ellie.

On the street in front of the Wilma, she took my hand. Her fingernails scratched my palm. "You have a car, right?" she said.

"Yeah."

"Get it," said Ellie.

I was afraid to leave her, afraid she would not be in front of the building when I returned. "Come with me," I said, but she shook her head.

"I'll be right here," she said.

My car was parked by the Higgins Street Bridge. As I walked down the metal staircase to the lot, my boots slipped on the ice. It was freezing, and I could barely see my way. I was apprehensive, but also filled with a strange excitement. I wanted a drink, too. I wanted many drinks. I was tired of being alone. Didn't I deserve a thrilling life?

It took two tries to start the car, but the engine turned over and I breathed on my fingers as I waited for the heat to kick in. I turned on the radio, and moved the dial until I found a Led Zeppelin song that suited my mood. I put the car in gear and drove up to Higgins. As promised, Ellie was waiting.

She climbed in the car and her skirt rode up her thighs. She rolled her head, rubbing her own shoulders. "I'm ready for some fun," she said. "Fuck Daven, you know?"

I nodded, though I did not know.

She directed me to take a right on Broadway. As we headed out of town, the lights were few and far between. Finally, she told me to turn into a bar called the Trail's End. There were a few beat-up trucks in the parking lot. I pulled the Wagoneer up to a snow bank and turned off the engine.

"Here we are," said Ellie.

"The Trail's End," I said, attempting to sound cheery.

Ellie kicked her door open and whirled her legs into the cold. She led the way into the bar.

It was a dim place, with a jukebox and Keno machines on the right and a long bar on the left. A few men sat at the bar. One had oiled hair and a wet-looking gash in his cheek.

Ellie smiled at the bartender. He nodded warily. "Charlene," he said.

"Ken," she said, "this is my friend Caroline." I nodded. "She's buying," added Ellie.

"Hi," I said. I held up my purse.

"What'll it be?" said Ken, a short man with a bristly moustache.

"Whiskey," said Ellie.

"On the rocks," I said. He took the bottle from underneath the counter, filled two glasses halfway. Ellie and I sat on barstools and sipped.

"How about cigarettes?" said Ellie. I gave her the money, and she walked to the machine, choosing a pack and bending over a little too far to retrieve it. The man with the wound looked at her appraisingly.

Ellie and I lit up. The whiskey warmed my cheeks and stomach; we ordered more. "Daven's such an asshole," began Ellie.

I nodded.

"He won't let me go anywhere, or have my own money," she said.

"Is he…," I said. "Does he hurt you?"

She shrugged. "Nah," she said, half-heartedly. "I just want my own money, you know?"

"Hm," I said.

"The problem," said Ellie, "is that I love him. I really do. And if you love someone, what can you do?"

Here was a question I could not answer. I took a big sip of whiskey. The truth was that I had never loved anyone, other than my own family. This seemed so pathetic, all of a sudden. I wished I had taken more chances, and I began to look around the bar, hoping wildly for a chance to take.

"If you go get Cokes," said Ellie, "we can just buy the whiskey and make our own drinks."

Ken nodded. "Saves you some," he said.

I agreed that this seemed like a good idea, and went to the gas station down the street and bought a six-pack of Coke. When I returned, a man was sitting next to Ellie at the bar: Daven. He looked me up and down when I approached the table, Coke cans trailing from my hand. I thought he might tell me to go, but he gave me a disturbing smile and said, "Let's get a table, ladies."

We moved to a beat-up table in the corner. Daven bought a bottle of Jim Beam and set it in the middle, along with three greasy glasses. Ellie grabbed the Cokes and set to bartending, pouring very strong drinks. As I drank, I began to feel buoyant. I was glad to be in a shadowy bar in Montana. Perhaps this was where I belonged. In truth, it was not so different from Bobby's Bar.

Ellie started a story about a man she once fucked. (This was the way she put it.) She was pale and bony, but as she talked about seducing a friend's father, I could see how she might have been tempting once, when her hair was thick and her face round and healthy. Daven listened with his chin in his palm, his mouth curling at the edge. He saw some glow underneath the mess she had made of herself. She was telling the story to hurt him, but he looked as if the story turned him on. I didn't want to worry about why this was so.

It was easy: I stopped worrying. I drank. I lit cigarettes and smoked them.

Then Daven was talking about his childhood dog, Ohio, who was hit by a car. Daven told the story well, and it was clear that the memory of finding Ohio's body still haunted him. Ellie chimed in with a memory of a dog she had owned. Its name was Snowball, she said, and her father had let it loose in the woods when it tore up the furniture. She was seven years old, and had looked for Snowball for months, wandering in the woods near her house in Maine.

Snowball? Maine? What the fuck was she talking about? I made myself a whiskey straight. I stood, swaying a bit. "Who wants to dance?" I said.

There was laughter, and then Daven had me in his arms. The song was "Sexual Healing" by Barry White. Daven's body odor was strong. I sank my face into his shirt. Ellie joined us. She gave me a full glass. The whiskey was like water now, and went down easily.

EIGHT

from the desk of

AGNES FOWLER

Dear Johan,

Well, I really don't know what to say. When I got home from the library, the FedEx delivery slip was hanging on my doorknob. It was a very strange day (more later), so I was a bit apprehensive about what sort of package I might be receiving. I had not ordered anything. (Though I had almost–very late one night–called for the Amazing Pasta Pot, which enables you to pour hot pasta water right through the holes in the lid. Ingenious! But I refrained.)

I went inside and called FedEx, and they told me that someone would come right over with my package. I made a cup of tea and waited. After two cups of Earl Grey, I poured a glass of Old Crow, my father's whiskey. It was such a strange day, as I said before, and I opened my purse and took out the flyer.

Let me backtrack.

This morning, a student came into the InterLibrary Loan office. He was tall and blond, and carried a large metal mug, which he rested on the counter while he filled out the Search Card. "Need any help?" I said, from across the room, where I was secretively eating a raspberry Danish.

"Um," said the student. He looked confused by the ILL card. I sighed, and licked the sugar from my fingers.

"Put the title of the book on the first line," I said, in what I thought was a patient manner. I saw him begin to write. "And put the author on the second line," I said. He nodded, took a swig from his mug, and continued. I had reached the counter, and saw that the book he wanted was called *Using Fractals for Sedimentary Analysis*. Ugh.

"Just put your name, phone number, and e-mail address on the last line," I said. I smiled, and he looked up at me. His eyes narrowed for a moment. "Right there," I said, pointing.

"You totally look like the lady on the sign," said the student.

"Excuse me?"

"The sign at Charley B's," said the student.

Charley B's is a bar downtown. "What are you talking about?" I said.

"Forget it," he said. He handed me the card, turned, and walked away. The back of his T-shirt said, "You can ALWAYS re-take the test. You can NEVER re-take the party!"

How odd, I thought. I took the card, and I found the book at the University of Oregon library. The student would have his fractal information by Friday. The day passed slowly, with the boy's words turning in my head. We had a Teamwork Seminar at three, and it was long and awful. A man with a mustache made us write down adjectives to describe our co-workers. About me, people wrote: "friendly," "punctual," and "a real ham." Sheesh! Does no one sense my inner mystery?

So after the seminar, I left to go home. On the way, I took a detour to check out Charley B's. Don't ask me why: I parked. I went inside the bar, and it was smoky and loud, as I had known it would be. I stood there for a minute, in the doorway, watching people drink. And then I saw the bulletin board.

I walked closer, staring at the flyer. It was white, with a huge photograph blown up and the words MISSING ELLIE above it. Underneath the photo, the flyer said PLEASE CONTACT THUNDERBIRD MOTEL, ROOM 400 WITH ANY INFORMATION! My brain froze, like my fingers when I forget my gloves and have to run from the parking lot to the library. My brain felt numb. Numb, but waiting for the pain that was sure to follow.

I hooked my fingernail underneath the thumbtack that was holding the flyer to the board. The jukebox was playing "My Way" by Frank Sinatra. I smelled beer, and hamburgers from the grill in the back of the bar. I pulled the tack from the board, took the flyer, and folded it into halves, then quarters. I slipped it into my coat pocket. I had still not unbuttoned my coat.

The bartendress (or do you call them bartenders, regardless of their sex?) was looking at me. I touched the paper in my pocket. I turned, and left.

While I waited for the FedEx person to arrive, I took out the flyer again. I really didn't know what to think. The picture was of me, Johan. It was the picture from the Arlee Pow-Wow and Rodeo. But who in the world was Ellie?

A FedEx woman with a perm arrived at my house with an enormous package. Johan, it was from you. I signed the "received" slip, and brought the package inside. I opened it with shaky fingers. It was quite a day, as I have mentioned.

The sun lamp is just wonderful. It looks a little overwhelming, but I do hope that, as the instructions promise, it raises my levels of serotonin and makes me a more contented person. It was very thoughtful of you, Johan (if not exactly romantic). I hope the lamp works quickly. I would like to feel more contented, Johan, because right now what I feel is scared.

Sincerely,
Agnes

NINE

I WOKE UP NAKED in my bed, filled with regret for something I couldn't place. There was a piercing pain behind my eyes. I began to cry, but I didn't know what for.

I covered my face. There were only shards of memory: kneeling on a floor, a tongue in my mouth. What had I done, before my fitful dreams?

I heard the phone ringing in the hallway. I was afraid to go outside. Had I hurt Ellie? Had I slept with someone? I was sore all over; I could not tell what had happened to my body. The phone kept ringing. Finally, I pulled on my robe. There was no sound in the building but the ringing phone. I picked up the receiver. "Care?" It was Ron's voice.

"Yes?"

"Care, it's the baby. She was born last night."

"What?"

"She's too early," said Ron quietly. "Only twenty-seven weeks."

"Oh God."

He sighed. "Maddy's tired," he said. "She's asking for you."

"Is the baby…is it going to…."

"We don't know," said Ron. "We don't know anything. She's so small, Care."

There was quiet for a moment, and I could hear Ron breathing on the phone.

"Oh God," I said again.

"I guess…," said Ron. "I thought…you'd come home."

"Oh Ron," I said. "I don't know."

He didn't say a word. I didn't even hear him breathing. I heard a click; he had cut the line.

In my apartment, I closed my eyes and slipped back into dreams: I was pulling up to Maxwell Elementary in my parents' Oldsmobile. Ellie was waiting this time, and she ran to the car and climbed in. We drove through downtown to I-95 and headed south, toward New Orleans. "Thank you," Ellie said, her eyes so large and trusting, her face lit by passing headlights. "Thank you for saving me," she said. I reached for her, but she turned to dust in my arms.

In the back seat was Madeline, who had been there all along.

The phone in the hallway rang again, and I went and answered it. "Ron?" I said.

"Olivia?" said a ragged voice. It sounded like an older man.

"I'm sorry," I said.

"Is that you, sweetie?" said a woman's voice. She sounded

hysterical.

"This is Caroline," I said.

"Who?"

"Caroline," I said. "I'm Caroline."

"Where's our daughter?" said the woman.

"Look. We know she's there," said the man. "We traced the call. Put her on the phone, goddamn it."

"I don't...."

"Olivia!" cried the woman. "Where's Olivia?"

"I don't know," I said.

"Where are you?" It was the man again. He sounded both angry and terrified.

"I'm in the hallway," I said.

"We're coming to get our girl!" the woman said, and she burst into tears.

"Where is this phone located?" said the man angrily. "We'll find out on our own, young lady, you know we will."

"The Wilma Building," I said. "Missoula, Montana."

"Jesus Christ," said the man. "Missoula fucking Montana."

"Where's Olivia?" cried the woman again.

"You tell my daughter we'll be there in the morning. You tell her to stay put."

"I don't know–" I said, but the line had gone dead. I heard a door open, and I looked up.

Ellie stood in her doorway. She wore boxers and a dirty bra. Her eyes raged; her face was sunken. Her right arm was marred by a large bruise. "Hello," she said.

Finally, I knew it was over. Olivia stood in her doorway.

"Your parents are coming to get you," I said.

"What are you talking about?"

I just looked at her. I didn't say a word.

"Fuck you!" she screamed, her hands in fists, fighting the air.

I almost went to her. I almost took Olivia into my own apartment, helped her come down from whatever she was on, sang her to sleep until morning, when her parents would come for her. But something had changed in me.

I turned my back on Olivia. I picked up the pay phone and I dialed. When Ron and Madeline's machine answered, I left a message. "I'm coming home," I said.

I packed my things quickly. It wasn't hard to see that the gown, the beanbags, the "Missing" posters, the coffeepot, and the grainy photograph of the Arlee Pow-Wow were things I could leave behind. I had one sister, anyway, and I had lost her for long enough.

TEN

He saw Isabelle in Forsyth Park, and knew her immediately from her languid steps.

"Isabelle?" called Bernard, and she turned.

Her face was lined, but she looked the same. She wore her hair short, and she was slim in a yellow suit. "Bernard?" she said. "My Lord!"

"What are you doing in Savannah?" he said, but did not say, why didn't you call me?

"My mother," she said, simply. She brought her hand to her neck.

"I'm so sorry," he said. "I heard."

She shook her head. "She had a good, long life. Your parents?" she said.

"Both gone."

For a moment, they were silent. It was March, and the azaleas were in full bloom. Sunlight poured through the oak trees, and tourists wandered past the dying mansions, snapping pictures. "It's been, what?" she said.

"Over twenty years."

She laughed. "It's hard to believe," she said. "I've got two daughters, now. Caroline's nine and Madeline is seven."

Bernard looked down. He did not say anything. "Did you marry?" said Isabelle. "Well, of course you did."

"We're divorced now."

"Oh." She stepped toward him.

"Why don't you come up?" said Bernard. "We'll have tea."

She paused only a moment before nodding. They walked toward Jones Street, then up the stairs. She sat close to him on the couch, and told him about her failing marriage, about Joseph's drinking. "Maybe I made a mistake, leaving you," said Isabelle. "Maybe I should have married you after all."

It took three cups of tea, half a package of Little Schoolboy cookies, pimento cheese on Triscuits, and a bottle of sherry, but finally their lips met again.

ELEVEN

from the desk of

AGNES FOWLER

Dear Johan,

My mother died when I was five. I remember some things about her: her warm arms around me, the way she hummed as she brushed my hair. I don't think about my past, because it makes me feel out of sorts. And life is hard enough already, don't you think? Perhaps the sunlamp isn't doing its job.

When I was five, my mother died, and my father and I stayed in a hotel room. I remember pushing my face into a pillow and crying. My father cut my hair with clippers, and I can still feel the metal teeth on my neck. When I think about this, I can't breathe. My father told me I was upset about my mother. He told me to be quiet. I was the light of his life, have I said that? I was everything and why would I want to hurt him when he had given me his truest self? Just be quiet, just be quiet, and know that I love you, Agnes, so very much.

Johan I am writing so fast that my hand is hurting. Please forgive the rip in the paper. I just need to get this out. My hair was short, like a boy. He took me to the airport. Our flight to Montana was late. I had to go to the bathroom, but he wouldn't let me. We sat in a corner, away from the gate. I watched the planes arrive and depart. They rushed down the runway and then lifted into the air. My father stood behind me, his hands on my shoulders, and I had to go to the bathroom. I was in the wrong place, and I watched the planes at LaGuardia Airport. They rose higher and higher and then they were in the clouds.

On the plane, he let me go to the bathroom. I looked at myself in the mirror. I touched my short hair. I looked like a boy but I was Agnes Fowler. I was the light of my father's life.

When we reached the house in Montana, there was my room. I didn't remember it, but there it was: a small bed with a handmade quilt, a bookshelf filled with books. I did not have any clothes, but my father took me to the Salvation Army and bought me a closetful. My coat and my shirts smelled like other kids, not me. He had already given away all my mother's clothes, he said. There was only a strand of pearls left, which he kept in his top dresser drawer.

On his desk and on my bedside table, there was a picture of my mother. She was beautiful, a young woman with blond hair. Her shoulders dissolved into smoke. I knew her. At night, I could hear frogs. I kissed the picture of my mother.

My father worked in the lumberyard. He came home every night right after work. I had his love to myself. When

I was older, I wanted him to find a girlfriend, so I could go out on a date, or to the movies. But he told me I was all he wanted in the world. It felt good, to be loved so much. He was afraid if I was even an hour late. When I walked in the door from school, he would grab me in a bear hug.

Johan, I would like to come and see you in Alaska. I am not feeling very well, and I think a change of scenery might be just the thing. My house is starting to feel cramped, and though I used to spend hours reading or doing crossword puzzles in the evening, now I have the feeling that someone is watching me through the window. Of course, no one is watching me. Don't get me wrong, Johan, I'm not a loony! I just think that March in Alaska might be something to see. Is it light all the time yet?

Let me know. I have been looking online, and tickets to Anchorage are not too expensive. How far is Skagway from Anchorage? Can one fly into Skagway?

I must admit, at first the word "Skagway" didn't thrill me. It sounds like a slang word for marijuana, like "Mary Jane" or "doobie." But now I'm getting used to it. Let me know what you think, anyway. I don't want to rush you, but as I said, I'm feeling the need for a break.

Oh. One more thing. I went over to the Thunderbird Motel. I asked for the room on the "Missing" flyer. Better to know the whole story, I decided, than to just wonder about it. Well, the room was vacant. It was the honeymoon suite, turns out. Someone was there, but now they've checked out.

The front desk clerk, who everybody calls "Elvis" (needlessly flattering him, I think), told me the name of the girl:

Caroline Winters. Why would someone named Caroline Winters be looking for me, I thought. I knew something had gone wrong. That's really why I want to visit, Johan. It's not the house, and it's not the crossword puzzles. I hope you can read my words. My hand is shaking a bit so just hold on, will you?

Have you ever had a hot toddy? Oh, they are just delicious. I'll make you one someday. Actually, I'll enclose the recipe. You can make one right now if you'd like. Why don't you? That's sort of romantic. Make a hot toddy, and we'll continue.

First, put the kettle on. Next, put a spoonful of sugar in a mug, and a bit of water, enough to make the sugar dissolve. Then add a jigger (or two) of whiskey or Scotch. (Old Crow works just fine.) Now fill the mug with the boiling water from the kettle, and grate a bit of nutmeg on top.

Take a big sip.

OK. So I feel like I'm in another life. Like there's another me, or something. I once read about a scientist in a wheelchair who studies black holes and other such pheonomena. (How do you spell phenomena?) One thing he believed is that as we go along, our lives split sometimes, into other lives. Like the other day, I drove by the Humane Society, and I almost went in and got a dog. I thought about it, how nice it would be to have a dog at my feet, bringing me the paper. But I didn't drive in. I drove past the Humane Society, and to the Orange Street Food Farm.

So what this wheelchair-bound scientist (and he was a randy fellow, as I remember—dumped his long-suffering wife for his buxom nurse) said is that when I decided not to turn into the Humane Society, my life split. In one life, I *did* pull in. I picked out a nice scruffy dog—perhaps a St. Bernard—and then I brought that dog home, and didn't stop at the Food Farm at all. (Though who knows what I had for dinner! Maybe rice.) In other words, there are all these lives, and they are all mine, but I'm only aware of one of them. This one, the one in which I'm alone and drinking a hot toddy, writing to you.

Well, what the hell. Here's what happened after Elvis told me the name "Caroline Winters." I went to the Cyber Café on Higgins Street, and I paid for a half-hour on a computer. I went to Google, and I typed in "Caroline Winters." After a few wrong clicks, I came upon an obituary from the *Holt Record,* a newspaper in New York. I clicked it. It was all about Caroline Winters' mother, a woman named Isabelle Winters. She died in a car crash on New Year's Day. She is survived by her daughters, Caroline and Madeline.

I had an extra dollar. I printed out the obituary, and I took it home. Make another hot toddy, Johan, because here is the kicker. They had a big picture of Isabelle Winters in the obituary in the *Holt Record.* I sat in my father's chair, and I held the picture to my face. I wished I had a dog. I think I am going crazy. I held the picture to my face, did I say that? It was the same picture, Johan. The same picture on my bedside table. The one on my father's desk. The woman with the pearls. My mother. Her name was Isabelle Winters, and she is dead.

A.

TWELVE

I FOUND RON on the third floor of the Neonatal Intensive Care Unit at Mount Sinai, staring at a tiny pink creature in a glass box. I stood by his side, and it took him a moment to notice me. "Is she beautiful?" he asked, "or is it just me?"

I looked at the tiny thing. She was no larger than a melon, and her head was too big. Her skin was a strange red color–it was loose on her bones. Wires and tubes snaked along her body. She had a tuft of white-blond hair. I was overwhelmed with my feelings for her: I wanted desperately to cradle her. The wind was knocked out of me. "She's beautiful," I said.

"Her name is Isabelle," said Ron.

"After Mom," I said.

He turned to me. His eyes were ringed with circles. "She's almost three months early. They say she might not...," he said.

"Don't listen to what they say."

Madeline was asleep when we approached her bedside, but she opened her eyes when I touched her arm. "You're here," she said. She sounded surprised, and my heart hurt for all the times I had let her down.

"I'm here," I said.

She exhaled a long, low breath. "Isabelle," she said, "after Mom."

I smiled. My sister looked so fragile in the metal bed; her hair was tangled and her eyes clear. Her face was swollen. "Was it awful?" I asked.

"Oh God," she said, and she began to cry. "I don't think...," she said, and then she stopped.

"Madeline," I said, "you did a beautiful job. Isabelle's here, and she's going to make it. We're going to take her home, and put her to sleep in Nana's bassinet."

She smiled, but shook her head. "You're the one who believes in miracles," she said.

In the cafeteria, Ron and I drank coffee. "So where's your other sister?" he said, tightly.

"It wasn't her," I said, knowing finally that it was true.

"I'm sorry," said Ron.

I sighed. "Time to let her rest," I said. He did not ask if I was talking about Madeline or Ellie. He did not respond at all.

"Let's go see Isabelle," I said, and he nodded.

In the glass box—it was called an incubator, I found out later—my niece fought for breath. "There are some things you should know," said Ron.

"Oh," I said.

"I've been laid off."

"Ron, I'm sorry," I said.

He shook his head. "I don't know how I'll take care of them."

"Ron," I said.

"I took some chances, and made some stupid investments. I'm such an asshole," he said. But I saw the way Ron looked at his baby daughter. I knew the way he cared for my sister, the way he loved her. He was even looking out for her now, asking me to stay around, asking me to help.

"You're not an asshole," I said.

THIRTEEN

MADELINE CAME HOME after a few days, but baby Isabelle had to stay in the hospital. They fed her Madeline's breastmilk through a tube.

I loved my niece fiercely. She had little control of her limbs, which thrashed in all directions. Every rise and fall of her chest filled me with wonder. We started calling her "Bella" or "the Bean." I slept on Ron and Madeline's couch, and spent my mornings at the hospital. In the afternoons, I walked around New York City, smoking cigarettes and letting the live-wire energy of the city into my skin.

One morning, the nurse told us we could bathe Isabelle if we wanted to. Madeline looked at me. "Why not?" I said.

"Right," she said. "Why not?" She looked exhausted to the bone. Ron stepped back from the incubator. He was scared, too.

The nurse, a tan woman named Renée, moistened a square of gauze and pinned it between two Q-tips, giving it to Madeline. "Reach in through the portholes," said Renée. Madeline reached toward her daughter, who was asleep in the incubator. "Just hold the gauze square with the Q-tips, run it over Isabelle," said Renée.

"What if I hurt her?" said Madeline.

I put my hand on Madeline's shoulder. "You're her mom," I said. This seemed to calm Maddy. She took a breath, and touched the gauze to Isabelle's skin. "It's hot in there," she said.

The nurse didn't say anything.

Madeline ran the gauze all over Isabelle, cleaning her. She was whispering something, a lullaby.

The nurse asked if Ron would like a turn. He was breathing hard, and then he said, "You know, I think I'll sit this one out."

When Madeline had cleaned every inch, the nurse moved in. "I'm going to turn her over now," she said. "But first, I'm going to unhook her ventilator."

When the ventilator was disengaged, Isabelle's oxygen saturation dropped quickly, and the oximeter alarm sounded. "Don't worry," said the nurse. She reached into the incubator and picked up Isabelle, who was so limp it seemed her parts were not connected. She turned her over, re-attaching the ventilator. The alarm stopped, and Isabelle's oxygen saturation climbed. Madeline was looking at me.

"Oh, no," I said. "I'll just watch." But Madeline did not make a move. The nurse held out the Q-tips.

I was frozen. I didn't want to reach inside the incubator. "I...," I said.

"Please," said Madeline. I stood there, in front of my sister. She had never asked anything of me, not really. Isabelle was on her back now, her head so big, her body so fragile. She was looking at me, too, but I couldn't do it.

"Why don't I finish up," said the nurse, finally. Madeline turned to Ron, and he took her in his arms. I could see from the way her shoulders moved that she was crying without sound. I tried to catch Ron's eye, but he was looking down, and stroking my sister's hair.

That afternoon, I walked by the entrance to a Steinway dealer. It was a huge hall, imposing, but I paused for only a moment before going in. A woman with her hair in a bun sat at a desk, reading through small glasses. She pulled the glasses off and looked up in an elegant motion. "May I help you?" she said, smiling.

"Oh," I said, "I just wandered in."

"Feel free to play," she said, and then she put her glasses back on and continued reading. I loved that she left me alone. In the back room, where all the pianos gleamed, I sat down at a mahogany baby grand that had been lovingly restored, touching the keys lightly with my fingertips. I thought of the names of songs—*Rhapsody in Blue, Moonlight Sonata, Für Elise*—but there were no notes in my head. The information was there, but not the music. I had lost it, somewhere between Montana and New York.

"Do you play?" The woman was standing next to me, one foot crossed over the other. Her glasses hung around her neck on a gold chain. She wore a blue-green dress made of a soft-looking fabric. It fell around her in waves.

"No," I said, "not really. Not anymore."

"Would you like to hear it?" she said, gesturing to the piano.

"Yes," I said. I stood, and she took my place. She pulled her hands into fists, let them go, and began to play Satie's *Gymnopédie #1*. The song filled the room. I closed my eyes.

She finished, and it was a moment before I opened my eyes. The woman was looking at me with concern. "Are you all right?" she said.

"I'm fine," I said brusquely. I walked quickly out of the showroom. Back on the street, I lit a cigarette. I was in the mood to drink, to meet someone strange and hot and spend the afternoon tangled up in the wrong thing. I couldn't stop seeing Isabelle's face looking out at me from her glass cage.

I found myself on a train, heading to Holt. I had bought a cold beer for the ride. The towns of my youth sped past: New Rochelle, Mamaroneck, Harrison. I tried not to think, though there was much to think about. What the hell was I doing with my life, for example. I was living with my sister, wearing her clothes. I had no job, a New Orleans apartment that was surely being infested with roaches, and I couldn't even bathe my tiny niece with a fucking Q-tip.

At the Holt station, I left my empty beer can behind and walked onto the platform. It was a sunny day. Madeline's jeans were tight on me, but not appalling, and the little Agnès B cardigan was downright cute. I had a cigarette while I walked to the Liquor Barn.

The store smelled the same as I remembered: dust and cardboard. I walked along the rows of stacked boxes, each full of wine. There were handwritten signs: WINE SPECTATOR TOP PICK: $9.99! BARGAIN BIN, ALL WINES $6. I remembered being shorter than the signs, only cardboard-level. I would stand in the back, by the gumball machine, while my father stocked up. He used one of the red plastic baskets, piling in Scotch and wine. Sometimes I checked the liquor cabinets at friends' houses when I slept over, to see if anyone else's dad drank a handle of Scotch a night.

I was startled out of my reverie when a short man wearing an argyle vest said, "Can I help you?"

"Oh," I said, "is Anthony here?"

"No," said the man.

"Oh, OK."

"Did you want some...." When I didn't speak, the man finished, "liquor?"

"Yeah," I said. "A nice bottle for a romantic dinner."

"A bottle of liquor?"

"Sure, or wine, maybe."

"The Ravenswood Merlot is delicious," said the man.

"OK, I'll take a bottle."

"Wonderful."

And it did seem wonderful. Here I was, a normal gal, buying wine for a romantic dinner. I decided I would bring the bottle to Maddy and Ron's apartment, and leave it for them to have a little quiet time alone. I could go to a movie, or a museum.

"Did you want to leave a note for Anthony?" the man

asked, as he rang up my purchase.

"Oh, should he be back today?"

"Sure. He's just over at Laura's," said the man, sliding my wine into a crisp paper bag. Laura? I decided she was a platonic friend.

"You could leave a note," he said.

"No, no thanks."

After an ice cream cone at Baskin-Robbins and two more cigarettes, I walked back to the train station, swinging my bottle of wine and feeling frisky. I peeked back into the Liquor Barn, but Anthony was not in sight. It was time to get back into the city.

As I rounded the corner, I heard a voice say, "Hey!" I turned, and in the alley behind the store was Anthony. "I thought that was you," he called.

"Oh, hey," I said.

Anthony walked toward me, wiping his hands on his pants. "What are you doing here?"

"Well," I said. "It's a long story."

"Yeah?" he said. I nodded. Then he nodded. This was going nowhere.

"I'm about to catch a train," I said, motioning with my wine bottle toward the station.

"What?"

"I'm staying in the city."

"OK," he said. He added, wistfully, "Well, it was good to see you."

"Yup."

"By the way, I'm so sorry about your mom."

I sighed. "Yeah," I said. After a minute, I said, "I keep forgetting. I keep thinking she's just at home." My voice broke. "I keep picking up the phone to call her." We stood there for a minute in the crisp evening. "You want to grab a beer?" I said.

"Well," he said. "OK, sure."

We walked to the Holt Grill and Bar. One beer turned into four, and then into dinner. Anthony was easy to talk to, and I told him everything. We talked and drank beer and then we went back to his house, on Mead Place. We drank the Merlot, and then some cognac. We laughed and I hadn't laughed in so long and he played the guitar and I sang and we fell into bed and tangled the sheets.

FOURTEEN

from the desk of

AGNES FOWLER

Dear Johan,

What can I say about hearing your voice on the phone? I could have listened to it all night. Your kindness came through loud and clear. I can't believe your nickname is "Boom Boom." And OK, I'll tell you why I chose you from all the other AlaskaHunks. Every one of them had a picture of themselves with a truck or a dog. Only you, my dear Boom Boom, had a picture with a cat.

I'm going to finish this note and then start packing. Now I know you said to pack a fancy dress, and warm boots and coat, and I have my fur hat that I got at the Bon Marché. And a bathing suit, though that seems just ridiculous to me. A bathing suit! In Alaska! This hot tub better be very hot, let me tell you.

I'm also packing some surprises, and some chocolates. I'm sure you have chocolates there in Skagway, but maybe not Godiva chocolates, which is what they sell at the Bon Marché.

I do have something to confess, Johan. You were right to be jealous of Snappy. I told you on the phone that you were being silly, but I'd like to begin our relationship with the slate wiped clean. And the fact is that after my sexy photo session, Snappy did come by the library, and he did not have a patron request. Au contraire! He wanted me to join him at the Annual Elk's Club Ball. And though I dearly wanted a reason to wear my mother's pearls, I said no. Perhaps there is an Annual Explosives Engineers' Ball?

By the way, Frances took the news of my sudden vacation rather well. I did not mention an Alaskan Hunk. I told her, instead, that I was going to see family. And I hope it won't scare the bejeezus out of you to hear this, Johan, but I didn't feel like I was lying. Should I have written that? Maybe not, but then again, what the hell.

I suppose you could say I'm throwing caution to the wind. My father always told me that he and I were alone in the world. When I asked why there were no pictures of other family members—no aunts, no cousins—he told me to shut up, and left me locked in the house. I have never seen a picture of myself as a baby.

When he came back from his fishing trip, he told me there had been a fire. My mother died in a fire, and everything of hers was gone, and there was only him, my father who adored me, and a house on Daly Avenue in Missoula.

A closet filled with Salvation Army clothes. I remember the clippers on the back of my neck in the hotel room. I remember being on a plane, and being scared. I did not try to tell my story any differently. He gave me a story and I took it. What choice did I have?

What choice do I have?

I want to make a new story, just start over. The story is: I saw you on AlaskaHunks.com, and I wrote to you. The story is: I am a librarian. I shop at the Bon Marché. I am the kind of person who packs a bag full of clothes, lies to her supervisor Frances, and hops on a plane heading north. I take chances. I move forward. Where I came from and whatever snarled stories lie behind me are of no importance. I start over when I need to. I am starting now.

See you tomorrow,
Agnes

FIFTEEN

On Bull Street, Bernard bought the perfect watch. It was slim and gold, and the numerals were elongated. It was decades old, the owner of the antique store told Bernard, and yet it worked perfectly. She'd have to wind it every day, and think of him. Perhaps he would wind it for her each morning, while he read the Savannah Morning News *and she slept upstairs. They would take the room that had been his parents'. He had lost a good deal of their money, but with Isabelle by his side, he could set things right. He had the watch engraved with the date and a few words.*

They were to meet at The Olde Pink House on Abercorn at seven. Bernard arrived early, ordered a martini. He touched the white tablecloth.

He had told her he'd been in New York on business, but he had lied. He didn't have much business anymore, without his father to hand it to him. He had gone to New York to seduce her again, and he'd been successful. He invited her to dinner, and then to his room at the Algonquin. Her skin was yielding, and she still smelled of caramel.

*

He wasn't right in the head anymore, said his ex-wife, with her lawyers, her restraining orders. He looked too long at little girls, she said. As if strolling by a schoolyard was a crime!

Isabelle should come back home to Savannah, he told her, imagining the life they should have had, together. He hadn't thought she'd say yes.

At seven-fifteen, he ordered sautéed shrimp with ham and another drink. The waiter, Henri, was a friend. He brought the plate out steaming, and made to take away the second place setting. Bernard stopped him, holding up his palm. "She's late," he said, "but she'll be here."

He dipped his fork, bringing a shrimp to his lips. The sauce smelled of butter.

At seven-thirty, he drank another martini, and ordered the grouper stuffed with crabmeat. Isabelle wouldn't like the Vidalia onion taste in his mouth. She had told him, wrapped in the terry cloth hotel robe, that she was miserable in her life. He was her angel from heaven, she said. She had been given another chance.

At eight, Bernard looked up at the chandeliers. He crossed his arms over his chest. Rage was a new emotion to him, but he was getting used to it. At eight-thirty, he paid the bill, sliding his credit card into the leather folder. He left a good tip: twenty-five percent. On the way out of the restaurant, he lit a cigarette.

A week later, he got the letter. The paper was thick, cream-colored. She wrote only five words: I couldn't leave my girls.

Bernard took the paper between his fingers and tore it into squares. He ripped it again and again, smaller and smaller until it was nothing but confetti. Then he threw it into the gutter.

SIXTEEN

ANTHONY AND I ATE TOAST, coffee, and Advil in his kitchen. I still liked him, even in the daytime. "Maybe you should come over for dinner tonight," I said, surprising myself.

"Over where?" he said.

"My mom's place. I can cook something."

"Can you?" Anthony raised his eyebrows.

"I can try," I said.

I called Madeline from my mother's condo. There was no answer, so I left a message. The condo was spooky, but once I lifted the drapes and dusted things off, it felt better. The realtor had shown it some, but Madeline was waiting for someone to pay top dollar. We weren't in any hurry, after all.

Madeline called me back from the hospital. "What are you doing there?" she asked.

"Long story," I said. "I'm really sorry I didn't call last night."

"Whatever."

"How's the Bean?"

Madeline sighed. "The same. I want to grab her out of that thing and take her home, you know?"

"Why don't you and Ron come out here for dinner?" I said. "I'll cook. Maybe it would be nice to get out of the city."

"I don't know," said Madeline.

"Well, think about it."

"I'm just feeling really down," said Madeline. "That damn Ken Dowland called again."

"Really?"

"Yeah." Madeline sighed. "I told him I wasn't getting involved."

"You did?"

"I just...after Mom died, I lost steam, I guess. It doesn't seem like the right thing to do anymore. Mom didn't want it, you know?"

"We can talk about it tonight. Come out for dinner. Anthony, um, from the Liquor Barn? He's coming, too."

There was a pause. And then, God bless her, Madeline laughed. "We'll be there," she said. "You, cooking for a guy? This I've got to see."

After I hung up the phone, I sat at the kitchen table. A longing came over me like a wave. I wanted to talk to my mother. I didn't care if we talked about Ellie, or the weather, or the cheese ball. There was so much I wanted to tell her: that I might be falling for Anthony, that little Isabelle had her blond hair, that the honeymoon suite at the

Thunderbird Motel came with a cheap bottle of champagne. I needed her to show me how to live through sadness, how to make someone dinner. All I knew was how to be lost.

SEVENTEEN

HER FAVORITE FLAVOR was peppermint chip, and though he had to stop at two different grocery stores, Bernard found a cardboard tub, and packed it into the cooler with extra ice. He would do anything to see that grin.

Their fishing rods were already in the canoe. They set off on the Bitterroot early, the moon still pale over the mountains and the sky just turning pink. They sang "Mr. Moon" as they baited the hooks, and she rested her head on his knee, waiting for something to bite.

It was hot by mid-afternoon, and their arms, already deeply tanned, took on a reddish tint. "Are you burning?" he asked.

"No," she said, "I'm just right."

He unpacked the lunch, and they ate slowly. He had cut the crusts off her peanut butter and bologna sandwich. He pulled the ice cream out—a surprise—and she shrieked with delight. They finished the whole tub with two cold spoons, their fingers growing sticky and sweet.

*

He felt a tug on his pole, but handed it to her, watching as she reeled the fish in. She planted her sneakers and pulled, her muscles taut with effort. She wore one of his baseball caps, and her hair was bound by a rubber band. Her ears stuck out just the tiniest bit.

"I'm losing it!" she cried, looking at him with an exaggerated grimace.

"You can do it," he said. He did not move to take over, but he watched her carefully.

"Ah!" she cried, reeling quickly, but the fish was too strong. She pulled a broken line from the water. Tears sprang to her eyes, and she brushed them away with the top of her fist. "Dammit!" she said.

"Hey," said Bernard, "there's always another chance." He took her shoulders in his hands, and looked into her eyes. She flinched, but just a little. "Agnes," he said. "There's always another chance to take what you deserve."

EIGHTEEN

I CAN COOK THREE THINGS: chocolate chip cookies, Kraft macaroni and cheese, and gumbo. I learned to make gumbo when Winnie won a free cooking class at the New Orleans Culinary Academy and offered to bring me along. We took the day off, met for Bloody Marys at The Columns, and attended the class in fine form. The teacher was named Slim, and as he mixed up a big pot of gumbo, we sipped Dixies and flirted outrageously. After eating, we took Slim over to Bobby's Bar, where he learned a thing or two about fried catfish from Carole and her Wednesday Fish Fry.

In my mother's kitchen, I called Winnie. "I'm making gumbo for the Italian," I said.

"Damn, girl!" she said. "Where's Slim now, do you think?"

"No clue. Listen, I need you to read me the recipe."

"You think I still have that handout?" she said.

"Can you look?"

Winnie sighed dramatically. "I'll call you back in ten,"

she said. I made coffee and waited for the phone to ring, twisting the cord around my finger. I added a spoonful of sugar from my mother's bowl.

As she had predicted, Winnie no longer had the recipe. "But I do have Slim's digits," she crowed. "They were still in my wallet. I called him and got you the gumbo info."

I wrote it all down, and then Winnie told me about her new job at a snooty restaurant in the Marigny called Blue. "They've got blue martinis, blue beer," she said, "Now I'm all about ingenuity, but blue beer ain't right." She gave me the update on Peggy, who was still trying to break into modeling, but in the meantime worked at a lingerie shop called Nipple News. "She sells panties to her gal pals," said Winnie.

"The supermodels?"

"You got it."

"Wow," I said. "Have you been to Nipple News?"

"Hell, yeah," said Winnie. "Got a purple thong."

I shook my head. "Do you think Blue needs a piano player?" I asked.

"Are you coming home?" said Winnie. "It's about time."

"I don't know," I said, and I filled her in on baby Isabelle and Anthony.

"Sounds like you'd better stick around for a while," said Winnie. "Family's family."

"I guess," I said.

"And loving is loving. Damn!"

"Good point."

"Maybe I'll come see you," said Winnie. "Always wanted to take a bite out of the Big Apple."

"I'd love it," I said.

"Baby," said Winnie. "Have you given up on that sister of yours?"

I sighed. "She's either dead or she doesn't want to be found," I said. "And it's the same thing, really. I mean, it's not for me to save her, you know?"

"Yeah," said Winnie. "You have to take care of your own self."

"I guess so."

"Have some of that gumbo for me," said Winnie.

"I will," I said, and when I hung up the phone I felt lonely, as if something was over.

I rode my mother's bicycle to the A&P and bought everything on Winnie's list. They only had frozen okra and canned Ro-Tel tomatoes. I slipped a package of condoms into the basket.

I put on some show tunes and began cooking. I shelled shrimp, chopped chicken, sliced sausage, onion, and pepper. I put garlic through the garlic press. Before long, the kitchen smelled wonderful. As I cooked, notes came into my head, and when the gumbo was simmering, I sat down at the piano.

Over the years, my mother had gradually turned the piano into a glorified table, covered with framed photographs of us as children. After Ellie disappeared, nobody took pictures for years, as if snapshots would only capture the empty space between us, where Ellie should have been.

I lifted the keyboard cover and ran my fingertips over the keys. Finally, I played, the song in my head spilling out.

It was a sad song, and it needed work, but I resolved to get some composition paper in the morning. When I stopped, I was dizzy, and I realized I had been holding my breath.

I took a shower, toweled off, then used my mother's hair dryer and brush, her lipstick. In her mirror, I looked happy. She would have been proud of me, or at least my hair.

I couldn't stop myself from opening her desk. The folders of failed searches for Ellie were right where I had left them, in a neat pile. I flipped the top one open. *Isabelle Darling,* read a letter from my mother's Aunt Betty, *we are all heartbroken about your loss. I cannot believe it has been a year. Please know that if I thought of any lead, I would call you immediately. You don't need to remind me, dear. Bernard is still traveling in Europe; last I heard he had phoned his mother from an island in Greece. Kim's divorce is almost finalized, poor thing. She won't get to keep the house, and has moved with the boys to an apartment in Thunderbolt. Why don't you bring your girls down for a visit? You know you are more than welcome at Vernon View–I would appreciate the company.*

I pulled the next letter out: *Isabelle, I still think about your missing daughter every day. I pray you will find her, and do know that I will be on the constant lookout. I hope you are enjoying the spring in New York, it is quite hot here. You know that I love you, XXOO.* The letter was not signed, though it was clearly from an old friend or relative of my mother.

My first instinct was to sink to the floor and keep reading. But Anthony, Madeline, and Ron were due to arrive. I had a table to set, and a dinner to finish. I felt that my mother was guiding my hand to do something she was never able to do, during the long nights she spent alone in her condo: I took the folders and threw them in her bedroom trashcan, which was appliquéd with sailboats.

NINETEEN

from the desk of

AGNES FOWLER

Dear Johan,

Well, I'm not at the Skagway Airport, but I suppose you've noticed that by now. I should have arrived ten minutes ago, and we should have been on our way to your favorite restaurant, the one with the best steak in Alaska. There would be a bottle of wine waiting for us, or some mugs of beer, anyway. Maybe you would be kissing me.

I hope you will understand that this is not goodbye. I did not change my mind about you, in the Seattle Airport. Let me write it all down, and maybe it will make some sort of sense.

The flight from Missoula to Seattle was uneventful. My stewardess was snippy, giving me a cup full of ice and only a splash of ginger ale to cover it instead of the whole can. The view from the window was breathtaking as we headed up and out of Missoula, which I've always thought of as my home.

Have you heard the story of Cynthia Ann Parker? We learned about her from a History textbook. Cynthia was the nine-year-old daughter of Texas settlers. She was taken by the Comanche Indians during a raid. They raised her as an Indian, and when her parents finally found her twenty-five years later, she had already married a member of the tribe and had three children. She didn't want to go back to the white world. When she was forced to, she starved herself. In the book, this was a triumphant tale, a woman who knew where she belonged. It always seemed heartbreaking to me. It was too late, you see, for Cynthia Ann Parker to change her story. But it's not too late for me.

In the Seattle airport, I ordered a complicated coffee drink called a Mocha Frappucino. It was quite delicious. I checked the screen for my flight to Anchorage, and then I saw the flight to NYC/LGA.

It's easy to find someone, as it turns out. I went to one of the gleaming pay phones, and I called information. I asked for Holt, New York. I asked for "Winters." I got a phone number and an address, and I wrote them down with this very pen on the back of a receipt from the Orange Street Food Farm. (Thomas Regular Muffin-6 C; 1% Milk Gal; ENT Raspberry Danish Twis; Prem Froz OJ; Mozzarella Cheese; Keebler Cinnamon Crisp.)

There it was. An address, so simple. I figured I could take a cab from the airport to the address, and see what, if anything, was waiting for me.

Johan, I will come and see you. I just want to know more about where I've been, before I start thinking about where I'm going. They've dimmed the lights, and the man next to me has nestled into his square airplane blanket. His breathing is slow. Perhaps he's asleep already. The movie is *Just Married,* which does not seem to warrant the four dollars they're charging for headphones. (Criminal, if you ask me!) I ordered a little bottle of white wine, and I'm sipping it and looking out at the sky.

This feels like the plane I should be on. I think I'm going in the right direction, though I'm scared to death. God knows what I could be getting myself into, flying willy-nilly around the country.

Johan, I believe that sometimes you have to take a leap of faith. It wasn't so hard, after all, to approach the airline desk, look the attendant in the eye, and say, "LaGuardia."

Agnes

TWENTY

AT SEVEN, the phone rang, and Mitchell from the guardhouse said, “Anthony Sorrento for you, miss.”

“OK,” I said.

Anthony held a bouquet of wildflowers and a bottle of wine, and as soon as I took them, he wrapped his arms around me and squeezed.

“I'm just finishing dinner,” I said, flustered, when he let me go.

“I'll help you,” he said. But instead of heading for the kitchen, he pulled me in toward him again. I stayed there, feeling safe, feeling warm.

We wrapped hot sourdough bread in a napkin, and put butter on the dish. I set the table with my mother's silver—even the candelabra, which Anthony showed me was kept in the sideboard. “Your mother had a lot of parties,” he explained, sheepishly. “Sometimes I'd come early and help her set up.”

The gumbo was ready when Ron and Madeline arrived. Sliding glass doors led from the kitchen onto a balcony overlooking the driveway, and I saw Ron and Madeline's car pull in; they had negotiated Mitchell and the guardhouse without a phone call.

I met Madeline at the door. "Hey," she said, when I hugged her. She accepted the embrace, but reluctantly. "Look who's glowing," she said. I gave her a kiss on the cheek, and led her into the dining room.

Anthony took over in the kitchen, ladling bowls of gumbo and rice. I poured wine and sat down next to Madeline. "Did you make him cook?" she said disapprovingly.

"He's just helping. How's Isabelle?"

"A little better, maybe," said Madeline. "I don't know. She's stable. She's growing."

"She's amazing," I said.

Madeline's face lit up. In her eyes, I saw the girl she had been, always seeking my approval. I put my hand on my sister's. "Listen," I said.

"What?"

"I'll stay in New York, if you want me," I said. Madeline focused intently on her napkin. I sipped my wine. I felt irritation rising. Madcline was silent, and I wanted to take the promise back, to tell her I had places to go, anyway, and didn't need to hang around helping her. With effort, I kept quiet.

"Caroline," she said, "I do need you. I will need you. Thanks."

I took her hand and kissed it.

Over dinner, Anthony told us about the liquor store, which wasn't doing well. "People are buying at Sam's Club and

Costco," he said. "Mom-and-pop stores are becoming obsolete." He took a big bite of gumbo. "I have some ideas, but they don't talk about running your dad's store in school."

"Did you go to business school?" asked Ron.

Anthony shook his head. "Hotel school," he said. "I'm hoping to open a restaurant someday."

"I wish I knew what I wanted to do," I said.

"What about playing?" said Madeline.

"Playing what?" said Anthony.

"She used to play piano," said Madeline. "She was going to go to Juilliard."

"I didn't know," said Anthony.

"You were so good," said Madeline. "I always wanted to be that good. Remember my recorder?"

I laughed. Madeline had practiced her recorder night and day, but had never been able to master "Frère Jacques."

"Our life wasn't all bad," said Madeline. "You seem to want to think it was. But there were good times, too." Madeline was speaking only to me, and Ron and Anthony fidgeted.

"I'm trying," I said.

Madeline smiled. "I know."

"I wanted to play the drums," said Anthony.

"Violin," said Ron.

Madeline laughed. "I never knew that!"

"I was so bad," said Ron, "that the teacher asked me not to really touch my bow to the strings during the Christmas concert. I stood there and moved my arm back and forth, but never made a sound. My mother was so excited, and I felt like a total jerk."

We ate and talked, and the evening slipped by. Anthony asked to see pictures of little Isabelle, and Madeline pulled out her purse. I went into the kitchen to find the cookies. I touched Anthony's shoulder when I walked by him, and he brought his hand up to cover mine. I saw Madeline exchange a look with Ron.

As I arranged cookies on a plate, the phone rang. The clock read ten-thirty. I picked up the phone, and said hello. It was Mitchell. "Woman in a taxi here to see you," said Mitchell.

"What?" I said.

I heard murmuring, and then, "Agnes Fowler here to see you, miss."

My mouth was dry. I could feel my tongue in it, a heavy thing. "OK," I said, hanging up the phone. I unlocked the glass door and walked outside, onto the small, second-story balcony.

It was dark and hazy, but the porch light illuminated part of the driveway and part of the lawn. A taxi came to a stop in front of the condo.

A woman stepped from the taxi, then turned her face to me.

"Someone's here," called Madeline, from the dining room. Her voice was suffused with wine and laughter.

The air smelled salty, and I could hear the lapping of waves. I squinted to see the woman through the fog. Around her neck was a string of pearls. For a moment—but just a moment—I thought she was my mother.

I stood on the balcony, feeling the breeze against my face. I gripped the railing. "The door's open," I said, at last.

ACKNOWLEDGMENTS

Thank you, Kate Cantrill, Emily Hovland, Juli Berwald, Wendy Wrangham, Jill Marquis, Ellen Sussman, Anne Ursu, Michelle Tessler, Pilar Queen, Joe Veltre, Michael Carlisle, Clare Conville, Clare Smith, David Poindexter, Anika Streitfeld, the Meckel family, Laura Barrow, Sarah McKay, Liza Ward, and beloved Tip and Ash, who listened to me read this book all the way from Maine to Georgia.